Acknowledgements

First and foremost, I'd like to thank Jess Ross, Kirsty Carson, and Shawn Connor for reading early drafts of this novel, giving me their thoughtful critique, opinions, and suggestions for improving the story, characters, and structure.

I would also like to thank advance readers for helping with the launch of this book. These readers are Heather Miller, Manda (bearpiglovesbooks), Erin Anthony, Erica Wiggins, Emily Terry, Pan (undead_dad_reads), Michael R. Goodwin, Julia Lewis, Adam Kennedy, Jennifer Dockery, Megan Wilcox, Caleb Jones, Tylor James, Karla Kay, Todd Young, Saffron Roberts, Paul Preston, Liana Hubert, Shane Norton, Jessica (readswithfoxes), and Andi Finnell

Lastly, I would like to thank the bookstagram community for their eternal support, enthusiasm, and infinite love and patience.

The Modern Prometheus

Copyright © 2022 by Jayson Robert Ducharme

All rights reserved. This book or any portion thereof may not be reproduced or used in any manner whatsoever without the express written permission of the publisher except for the use of brief quotations in a book review or scholarly journal.

First Printing: 2022

Edited by Briana Morgan
Cover Art by Francois Vaillancourt

THE MODERN PROMETHEUS

A Novel

Jayson Robert Ducharme

The Modern Prometheus

Jayson Robert Ducharme

I.
BIRTH

"Nothing contributes so much to tranquilize the mind as a steady purpose, on which the soul may fix its intellectual eye."

Mary Shelley

1.

"...Peter—an you—hear me?

"You ne—o this for—

"—me..."

2.

It was a voice, somewhere far off, like an echo across a canyon. *My name?* Peter thought. *Someone is calling for me.*

He was falling—at least, it *felt* like falling—in some vast nothingness. When he tried to call back to that voice, he gagged. No words came out beyond garbled grunts.

A response: "Can you hear me?"

Yes! Peter wanted to cry. *Please help me! I don't know where I am!*

"Your vitals are dropping. Peter! You—got to hold—gain—el tha—cking thing..."

3.

The old cliché goes that you can see your life flash before your eyes when you're about to die; in this case, it was random and jumbled snapshots of life that appeared without cohesion.

There he was, six years old, running around the parking lot of his old apartment building in North Andover on a hot summer day. He was pretending to be a monster, chasing his baby brother Owen around. Peter gnashed his teeth and his hands clawed the air as his brother, wearing only a diaper, ran around screaming in excitement and terror.

Mom stood nearby with a hose, spraying down the car. Owen made a pass around the parking lot toward her, and with amusement she turned the hose to Peter, pressing her thumb against the nozzle, spraying him with cold water. Dramatically, Peter cried out and grabbed his face, staggering around like some great monstrosity taking a mighty blow.

"Take that, monster!" Owen cheered. "You'll never catch me! You'll—*ver catch—me—*"

"—PETER!"

Something slammed next to his head, rattling him. A powerful light penetrated his eyes.

"Look at me, Peter."

A shadow loomed over him like some extraterrestrial. Rubbery fingers pulled his eyelids, shining that light in. Everything was so cold. It was like he was submerged in ice.

"Dilation. Very good." The Shadow Man spoke directly to Peter's face, yet his voice was far away. "Can you hear me?"

What's happening to me? Peter tried to say but couldn't. *Where's Jack? Is he okay? I want to go home.*

"Shit! I'm losing you again! Why isn't this—"

The light faded. Peter found himself on his wedding day. It was held at a country club in Pelham with rolling knolls and little ponds that had fountains spewing water in the middle of them. It was the first hot day of the year after a miserable winter, and the clear blue spring sky beamed down on rows of white wooden chairs set up before a beautiful ceremonial arch decorated with white hydrangea.

Peter stood at that arch, wearing his best white suit and red tie. His bride-to-be Marjorie Strauss, done up in her best makeup and her hair stylized after Veronica Lake, came down the aisle with her mother, Helena. Margie's long flowing white dress lapped against the red carpet like dying waves receding against a beach.

Helena had a pixie cut and wore a purple dress. She smiled with pride at her daughter, and for a moment she cast Peter a knowing look—a look Peter was more than familiar with from

Helena Strauss. It was a *"you-better-not-fuck-up"* look. At any other time, that look would have made him anxious, but now, on his wedding day, she couldn't scare him.

Out in that crowd, Peter could see his own mother, dead now for several years, with her graying red hair and eyes lined with crow's feet. She was smiling at him with teeth showing. Mom rarely ever smiled, and it was even rarer to see her smile widely enough to see her yellow teeth.

His brother Owen sat with Mom, all grown up, in a pinstripe suit that he insisted on wearing, despite how silly it looked on him. Owen winked at Peter and shot him a finger gun, then wrapped his arm around Mom's shoulder and pulled her close. The Murphy family was very pleased.

Margie stood before him in front of the arch. She was smiling, but she was looking down at the ground, embarrassed by how emotional all this was making her. Every now and then, as the minister read off the vows, Margie would look up at Peter and her face would beam at him before she looked down again. When the minister permitted them to kiss, they embraced, and their lips met. They became husband and wife. The crowd all stood and applauded.

"*Peter*"—that voice permeated the memory—"I know you can hear my voice. Keep listening to me. Follow my voice, Peter. Follow me!"

Those rubbery fingertips pressed against Peter's eyes again and pulled them open. For a moment he could smell the breath of the Shadow Man. He was hyperventilating, and his voice was shaky with panic and excitement. *Tuna and lettuce*, Peter thought. That was what this man's breath smelled like, and it made him less of an abstraction.

"How many fingers am I holding up?" the Shadow Man asked.

Peter struggled to respond. When he tried to inhale, he felt cold liquid rise in his throat. Before he had a chance to fully articulate what was happening, the liquid was spewing out of his mouth, and a great pain emerged in his chest. He felt himself fall into convulsions.

"Shit!" the man said. "Hold on, god damn it! I've got you!"

Peter fell away again. He found himself rushing through the halls of Holy Family Hospital on September 15th, 2009. Sweat poured down his face, and as he ran, he unbuttoned his shirt to let his body have some air. It had been a long time since he had been this stressed and emotional.

Upon turning a corner, he saw Helena sitting in a chair with her arms crossed, nervously tapping her foot. The moment she saw Peter, she ran up to him and spoke with a displeased and frustrated tone. "Where have you been?" she said.

"Came here as fast as I could from the school."

"There's no excuse for you to be late like this."

Peter ignored her attitude. He knew that no matter what time he showed up, Helena would complain about something regarding him, but that didn't matter right now. Today was a big day, and he had far bigger things to consider than the animosity of his mother-in-law.

Peter followed Helena a few feet down the hall and they entered a labor room. Margie was lying in a bed with a doctor between her legs. Owen stood by the bed holding her hand.

"Christ, Peter, I thought you'd never show up," Owen said with relief.

Peter rushed to his wife and took her other hand. Margie gnashed her teeth and her eyes pleaded to him. He kissed her on the forehead and said, "I'm here."

He stared at the large bulge in her stomach. The doctor squinted as he focused on his work. A nurse stood next to him on standby.

"Not much more," the doctor said. "Just keep doing what you're doing, Marjorie."

Helena paced back and forth, scratching at her elbows while taking glances at the birth unfolding before her.

"Just a little more, Marjorie," the doctor said.

Within moments, a baby was heard crying. The atmosphere in the room eased, and everyone watched the doctor as he stood with a bright pink baby in his arms.

"She's here," he said.

Margie's eyes opened wide as the doctor brought the child to her. She took the baby in her arms and let out an exhausted, victorious sigh. Peter leaned over and looked into the baby's face. This was his child. This was *their* child. He could see it in her blue eyes, which looked like his, and in the mouth and nose, which looked like Margie's.

A hand clapped against Peter's shoulder, and he looked away from the baby at his brother's grinning face. "You're a real man now, Peter," he said.

Helena stared in astonishment at the family embracing their newborn baby with a look in her eyes that Peter had never seen before. Helena disliked Peter and had reluctantly supported her daughter's relationship with him. Yet now, with the way she was looking at him, Peter got the impression that to some degree she had finally accepted him, if only momentarily.

That had been the day Erin was born. That day he and Marjorie had begun a family.

"*I'm here, Peter,*" the Shadow Man told him. "*I'm almost there. Just hold on.*"

The memory rippled like a rock being thrown into a pond, and suddenly Peter could smell saltwater and suntan lotion.

"Don't get too close to the water, Jack!" Margie called. She was sitting on a towel in her two-piece red bathing suit, rubbing sunscreen on her arms. "Damn it. Peter, can you go help him?"

This memory—it had happened only last summer. Beachgoers sunbathed and paddled around in the waves. More people walked along the sidewalks with ice cream cones in hand, eyeing various shops featuring tie-dye shirts and hats that read "SUNNY FUN AT HAMPTON BEACH."

Little Jack was sitting near an unfinished sandcastle close to the water, not quite where the creeping waves could reach him, but close enough to where the sand turned gray and became sticky. He was crying loudly, grabbing his hand.

Erin, ten years old, came barreling up the beach in her one-piece pink swimsuit. The look on her face seemed not so much worry for her little brother, but concern that she had gotten in trouble.

"A bee!" she shouted as she ran up to Peter. "It was a bee that got Jack! We weren't doing anything wrong!"

"Settle down, Erin," Peter told her, setting his fold out chair next to where Margie sat on her towel. Jack had gotten stung before, so he wasn't concerned about an allergic reaction. "You're sure it was a bee that got him? That close to the water?"

"We were just building the walls for our castle when this big yellow son of a bitch attacked him!"

"Erin!" Margie pressed her knuckles to her hips. "What did I tell you about saying words like that?"

Peter chuckled, but it was a strictly outward expression. On the inside, his heart ached as he looked on at his poor boy, crying helplessly by himself. "I'll go fetch Jack."

The boy saw his father strolling toward him, and he got up and ran to him. Peter snatched the child up in his arms.

"Where's it hurt, Jack?"

With tears streaming down his cheeks, Jack held his wounded hand out. A white bulge emerged atop a swollen reddening mound on the knuckles. Swiftly, Peter plucked the stinger out of the wound and held it pinched before Jack's eyes to see.

"No little yellow son of a bitch is gonna hurt my boy," he told his son, flicking the stinger away. "Let's get you some medicine, Jackie."

The boy wrapped his arms around Peter's neck, squeezing him as if he were a life buoy.

"Is it bad?" Margie asked as Peter returned.

That voice again: "—*almost there*—"

"Jack will be just fine," Peter told his wife.

"*I've almost got you back, Peter.*"

The colors of the memory faded. The dark crept in like a tide and consumed him. For several moments, Peter thought he would be forever trapped in this limbo. And then, that familiar light returned, and Peter was carried up by some intense force toward it. There was no fear anymore. Everything seemed to come into focus. Peter accepted it.

"*You're back, Peter*," that voice said, clearer now than before. "*Magnificent.*"

May 17, 2021 was Peter Murphy's second birthday.

4.

Beep. Beep. Beep.

The sounds were dampened, as if he was hearing them underwater. It was some sort of machine, directly to his right. These sounds were the first thing he sensed upon emerging from that blackness.

When Peter finally awoke, he could feel nothing and could barely see anything. Colors swam in his eyes, finding no cohesion, and everything was dark and barely distinguishable. He was still unbearably cold. There was this peculiar disconnection between himself and his body. Then, he realized with relief that he was breathing. It was the stench that gave it away, because with each exhale, he could smell the vile and murky aroma of his breath.

Injured, I've been injured, Peter thought immediately. *I'm hurt and I don't know what happened to me or where I am.*

Footsteps approached. "Can you hear me? Anything? Perhaps you can read lips."

Who are you? The words vibrated in Peter's chest and tickled his throat but refused to come out. It was like paralysis.

The sound of scribbling was heard—a pencil against a clipboard. "Your throat. It's contorting. You're trying to speak, aren't you? Trying to respond to me?"

Why yes, I am trying to respond to you. SOMEONE GIVE THIS DUMBFUCK A PROMOTION!

"Listen, Peter…"

How do you know my name? Where am I? WHERE AM I?

"…I am a doctor. I'm here to help you. Let's try this. I'll ask you a series of yes or no questions. If yes, blink your eyes once. If no, blink twice."

Are my eyes even open? I think they are, and I can feel my eyelids moving, but everything is blurry and dark. Am I looking at a ceiling?

"Are you in pain?"

I'd rather feel pain than the nothingness I feel now. It was an endeavor, but Peter managed to blink twice.

More scribbling. "Do you know why you're here?"

Two blinks.

Yet more scribbling. "I won't press you with too many questions, Peter. I can tell that you don't have a lot of strength."

NO SHIT, EINSTEN.

"Do you remember what happened?"

Something certainly *had* happened to him, hadn't it? Otherwise, he wouldn't be here. He was alive and this wasn't some hell. If this guy says that he's a doctor, then Peter deduced that he must be in a hospital.

Did he remember what happened?

It was a struggle to recall the most recent memories he had. He knew that it was December, not long before Christmas. He had made a post online for his class to turn in their final papers on any subject regarding Irish literature. He remembered Margie in the kitchen, running her finger along the rim of her coffee mug, telling him that the pipes in the shower needed to get replaced. At one point Erin had excitedly showed him a painting she had done of a bird she had seen on the power line through her window. He remembered the lights of the Christmas tree in the living room, and how the tinsel glimmered in the dim evening light. And Jack—

Peter felt his tongue crawl into the back of his throat.

Jack… what's the last thing I remember with you, kiddo?

A memory of Jack playing with his wooden trains in the anteroom came to him. Another came where Peter was bathing the boy in the tub, and Jack had been pretending that he was making a storm by slapping the water. Yet, neither of these were his most recent memories of his son. His mind drew a blank. Something was wrong with his son.

Two blinks.

"One final question. Do you remember who you are?"

One blink.

A long pause came. No scribbling, just the sound of that repetitive beeping machine next to him. Peter's anger turned to fear. The hostility he felt towards this stranger became vulnerability.

Are you still there? he thought, despite knowing the question would fall on no ear.

"I see," the stranger finally said, then clicked his tongue. "I'll leave you be for now."

Please don't go. I don't want to be alone here.

The footsteps walked off, a door opened and shut, and then Peter knew that he was alone.

Please... I just want to know if my family is okay.

5.

There was light. Peter opened his eyes and found that he could see clearly again. A murky concrete ceiling loomed above him, glowing pale yellow from some unknown light source.

Wherever he was, it was hidden from the world, and it most certainly wasn't a hospital ICU.

Peter commanded his body to get up and move, but he couldn't get so much as a muscle to twitch. He then tried to move his neck but regretted it. A horrible pain seared the back of his head

"Uggnn."

Wait, was that...?

It was his *voice*. For the first time since emerging from the dark nothingness, he had heard his own voice. It was an absurd reassurance that he did, in fact, have a body. He wanted to hear it again, so he took air into his chest and managed a low vibration in the back of his throat: "Ugghnn."

A feverish nausea came over him. Despite being stationary, it felt like he was rocking side to side, as if he were in a ship on an unsettled sea. And then he felt it, coming up from his stomach. There was no gag reflex or resistance. A stinking liquid filled the back of his throat with a bitter taste, and then it spewed out of his mouth. No gagging or choking. Cold fluid swam down the sides of his face and into the fabrics of the bed he was on.

The liquid ceased rising, then it pooled into the back of his mouth and swam back down into his stomach. Never in his life had Peter wanted so badly to cry.

6.

A spider hung in the corner of the ceiling. If Peter directed his eyes to the left and slightly up, he could see it. It wasn't moving. Peter wondered if the insect was watching him.

The Shadow Man—that doctor without a face—hadn't appeared since he had questioned him. How long ago had that been? Hours? Days? It was difficult to tell. Peter floated in and out of consciousness, which only further complicated the matter of time. It isn't until you've been completely robbed of time—clocks, phones, sunlight—do you realize just how closely the structure of life is built around it. Little things stand out in ways that wouldn't normally when you have no perception of time, like the spider above him. Sometimes he heard pipes creak from water running, and other times he heard music, mostly classical, like Bach or Chopin, reverberating above.

Between the bouts of terror and confusion, his family possessed his thoughts. Margie, with her long dark hair, laying on their bed, telling him to come closer. How Erin would lock herself in her room for hours at a time, working on her canvas. And Jack…

He thought of Jack running around in his overalls and pointing at squirrels in the yard. He could still see Jack pressing his face against the living room window to watch Peter pull into the driveway after a long day of work. Little Jack, with his shaggy hair and tiny nose that went slightly upward like a snout.

Thinking about Jack upset him. Some deep paternal instinct ignited within him at the thought of his son.

7.

A cool wetness pressed against his temple. Peter's eyelids rose, and he could see the black visage of the Shadow Man sitting next to him out of the corner of his eye. He heard water dripping into something, and the Shadow Man reached over and dabbed a sponge against Peter's forehead.

"Thank you," Peter said.

The words shocked him. They had come out as a low wheeze, but they were distinguishable English words.

"You can speak?" the Shadow Man said. "And you're… working. Jesus Christ."

"Wha… hap-happen?"

The Shadow Man stood and loomed over him. The light in the room was still too dim to see him clearly, but it looked like he was wearing glasses. "Can you feel anything? Like when I touch your arm here?" he asked.

A vague sensation of pressure touched Peter's arm. "Little."

"Are you in pain?"

"Nausea."

The Modern Prometheus

"And you're aware? Conscious of your surroundings?"

"Where... my fam"—it was difficult to push the words out—"family?"

"You remember your family?" the doctor said, almost bewildered. "How much of yourself do you remember?"

Willing what little strength he had, Peter bawled: "Where ah th-they? Family! Mahgee! Jack! Eh-ren!"

The man hesitated to answer. "Your family is fine. I promise you."

"Lie!"

The Shadow Man stepped out of his vision. Footsteps fumbled out of the room.

"Guuhh b-buhh hurrr!" He wanted to scream, but he couldn't. The strain of it all was making him dizzy. "Gihhh... bahk!"

The door closed. Peter was alone again. He clenched his teeth and moaned. The rage he felt was impotent. He wanted to smash that insufferable beeping machine. He wanted to tear his hair out and kill this man keeping him prisoner.

Once the anger simmered, the Shadow Man's question pressed him: *"How much of yourself do you remember?"*

My name is Peter Kieran Murphy. I was born on July 30th, 1983, in North Andover, Massachusetts. That makes me a Leo. I'm thirty-seven years old. I'm a professor at Northern Essex Community College in

Haverhill, teaching English composition along with Romantic and Irish literature. I'm married to a wonderful woman named Marjorie Strauss, whom I met in college. We have two children: eleven-year-old Erin and two-and-a-half-year-old Jack. My mom is dead, and my father left when I was a baby. My dad was from County Cork in Ireland and my mother grew up in Lawrence. I have a brother named Owen in Lowell, and I live in Atkinson, New Hampshire. I'm a happy man. I'm a family man. I'm a man of academia.

The question of his identity was not up for debate. He knew who he was. He did not suffer from amnesia. The only thing he didn't know was what had happened to him, and why it somehow involved Jack. It was tearing him apart.

That spider lingered above. It was spinning a web. The frame and radial threads were completed, and it looked as if it was beginning the spiral that would entrap its prey.

I don't accept this, Peter thought. *I will not be trapped here.*

Peter closed his eyes. He focused all his attention on where he thought his right hand was. His jaw clenched and his brow furrowed as he strained to make it move. He felt the dim sensation of fingernails scratching against fabric.

Eureka!

It wasn't much, but he recognized the way it felt. He had a hand, and he could command it. It would just take time. Peter looked back up at the spider. *When I'm strong enough... I'll fight* back. *I'll get answers. What if that doctor is responsible for me being here? I'll make that son of a bitch pay.*

Just then, he realized something. It was his teeth, specifically the bottom row. Something felt off. Peter never had braces growing up, so a few of his teeth on the bottom row had come in crooked, namely the right premolar and the left incisor. Yet now, as he ran his tongue along the backs of his bottom teeth, they felt perfectly straight, and even seemed shorter than they were supposed to.

These are my teeth, he thought. *These… should be my teeth. Aren't they?*

8.

There was no peace in slumber. In his dreams, Peter chased his little boy through darkened labyrinths. Jack was always just a few inches out of reach. The child didn't even seem aware that his father was right behind him.

"Jack!" Peter cried. "Jack, wait!"

Yet the boy was always running, going around corners and vanishing. Sometimes Peter could reach out and feel his fingertips graze the back of the boy's overalls, but that was the closest he could get.

"Jack! Please!"

Something cold and foamy spread against Peter's face, and it jerked him out of the nightmare He opened his eyes, and out of the corner of his vision he saw the Shadow Man holding a shaving razor.

"Bad dream, Peter?"

"I want… my Jack b-back."

The man nodded. He dipped the razor into a bowl of water somewhere out of view—the water splash audible—then pressed it against Peter's cheek.

"Your speech is returning. Your body is also shedding flakes and growing fresh skin. You're getting hairy, too. Everything is starting to work as intended. This is all very good." He ran the razor down Peter's face. "You've also been conscious more often. Excellent progress. I've been thinking about providing you with some entertainment. I can roll in a TV, so you have something to watch while you continue your recovery."

A TV is a courteous gesture, but I would prefer BEING LET THE FUCK GO, PLEASE.

The Shadow Man continued shaving him in silence, then put the razor in the bowl, took a cloth and wiped the cream off Peter's face. "I want you to try something for me. I know it will cause some discomfort, but I want you to turn your head toward me."

Gritting his teeth, Peter turned his head to the right. He managed to move it at least an inch before the pain got too bad. He could see wires in the wall connecting to a large machine covered in dials next to his bed. The rest of the room seemed as barren and decrepit as the ceiling.

This is a basement, Peter thought grimly.

The Shadow Man was not so much a shadow anymore, and Peter caught a dubious glimpse of his face. He was clean shaven, had golden blonde hair neatly combed to one side, and thick round glasses that made his eyes look somewhat bugged out. He was young, probably not even in his thirties yet. He looked haggard and exhausted.

Seeing him, Peter felt a mixture of emotions: fear, confusion, and relief. Fear because he had no idea who this man was or what his intentions were; confusion because he seemed like he genuinely cared for Peter's well-being, but couldn't have cared if he was keeping him prisoner here; relief to just see another human being.

"We've already established that you have the memories of Peter Murphy, so I'll address you as such," the young doctor said.

Why the fuck are you talking like that? I AM Peter Murphy.

"I won't keep you completely in the dark, Peter. The past few weeks have been turbulent for you"—

Weeks? Did he just say weeks?

—"so it would be cruel to not at least inform you to some degree of your situation." He adjusted the glasses on his face. "My name is Dr. Jacob Abbott. I'm not here to hurt you. On the contrary, I'm here to keep you safe. I'm a graduate of Harvard and have received my doctorate from Johns Hopkins. You've suffered a terrible injury and I'm nursing you back to health."

"What… happen to… me?"

"You've suffered an enormous accident, but you're recovering. I'm keeping you safe in a secluded location. The police won't find you here."

Peter's eyes widened. "Police?"

"You don't remember anything regarding that?"

"No!"

The doctor pursed his lips in thought. "The police are looking for you, Peter. You're not safe anywhere except here. Do you understand? So long as you're with me, you're safe."

Peter's heart pounded hard enough for him to feel it in his ears. "What did I do?"

"I'm afraid I can't get into the details of what happened."

Peter felt the fingernails of his right hand digging into his palm. His body trembled and his mind erupted in panic. "What—happen?" he grunted.

The Modern Prometheus

"Peter, please!" Jacob stood and held him down. "Remain calm!"

"Out!" Peter's eyes bulged and words choked him. "Out! Out!"

The doctor took a syringe from his coat. He took the cap off the needle and flicked it with his fingernail. The sight of that needle sent Peter into hysterics. His mind demanded his arms to move, to grab this doctor and stop him, but they merely flopped by his sides.

The needle pricked his arm, and Peter floated away.

"I'll keep you safe." The doctor's words swam. "I promise you. You're safe."

9.

Laughter crept into Peter's head. When he opened his eyes, he discovered that the light was off, but there was a faint radiance against his bed.

"Oh Ricky, I didn't think that would happen!"

Peter craned his head to the right, ignoring the pain it caused him. A small old television was arranged on a fold out table. Within its black and white screen Lucille Ball wore a ridiculous looking hat while riding passenger in a car Desi Arnaz was driving. The laugh-track of the old comedy jeered at whatever the exchange was between the two.

Again, Peter didn't know how much time had passed. Again, he didn't know what the doctor had been doing to him in the time that he was unconscious. It was a loathsome thing to leave to the imagination.

I need to get control of my body back NOW!

Peter took a deep breath, and then focused on his arms. He felt them bend slightly at the elbow. With some effort, he pressed his elbows against the mattress beneath him and lifted himself up.

A white sheet was over him. He could see the landscape of his legs, feet, and torso beneath it. The rest of the room was too dark to see, but Peter suspected that it may have been just as nondescript as what he had already seen. He kept pushing himself up until he was in a sitting position.

Sweat dripped from his forehead. All of this was so much work. He squinted at the two mounds at the end of the bed that were his feet. As much as he tried, he couldn't get them to move. The toes on the right foot moved, but the left ones were still.

Arms are good enough for now, he thought. When he felt ready, he reached over to grab the sheet and pull it off but stopped himself just short of doing it when he saw his hand.

While his right hand seemed fine, his left hand was bandaged. It was covered from the fingertips to below the wrist. The fingers were gauzed together, rather than individually. Peter could feel them rubbing against each other when he wiggled them.

Seeing his hand like this made him apprehensive, but he couldn't pinpoint exactly why. *What are you so afraid of? You can feel your fingers, and they're working, so why the bandages?*

He began unraveling the gauze. The liberating sensation of air tickled his freed hand, like removing a band-aid after wearing it for several days. His hand was swollen and a little purple in spots. All around the wrist where the radius and the ulna bones met the hand itself was nasty stitching through bruised flesh.

Something was wrong.

Peter held both his hands before his face, examining them in the glow of the television light. His right hand was significantly larger and broader than the left, even with the swelling. The nails of the left hand were different as well, and the fingers were thinner. It was a woman's hand.

This isn't my hand. This is attached to me.

The realization came to him like a bullet. Slowly, his eyes turned to the shape of his body, and he tore the sheet off himself. He was wearing nothing except for his boxers—specifically the plaid ones that Margie had gotten him for his thirty-seventh birthday. Two tubes were attached to his torso. One was hooked to his abdomen above the belly button. The other was secured between two of his ribs just below the nipple.

His ribcage was visible through his thin and pasty flesh, and his stomach sank alarmingly inward.

"Oh Jesus Christ."

There was more stitching on his torso. It began at his navel, traveled up his abdomen and sternum, then split off into a Y shape across his chest to his collar bones.

"No—what is this?" Peter's fingers crawled through his hair. "What is this?"

More bandages could be seen on his left leg, just above the knee. His feet were different colors and sizes. The right one was white, and the left one was brown and an inch larger.

The terror could not be contained. It came out of him in an awful bellow, low and hoarse at first, then turning into a crescendo of agony. He screamed hard enough to rattle his ribs. His cries echoed off the walls and bounced all around him, filling the room. When it was finally out of his body, he broke down in hysterical sobs.

The laugh-track on the TV mocked him.

10.

Sleep didn't come for a long time. Peter lay on his bed, with only the light of the television to give him any semblance of comfort in the dark. He kept lifting his hand over his face—this hand that was not his hand—turning it front to back. He could see traces of purple nail polish on the middle fingernail. It became too much, so he wrapped the hand back up in its bandages and kept it under his sheet.

What else of me is gone? Are my organs still mine? My heart, my liver, my bones?

Part of him wanted to investigate his body further, but he felt that it was better not to. Again, he tongued the backs of his bottom teeth, and again he wondered if those teeth were even his. *I'm deformed. I'm disfigured. I'm a freak. So much of me isn't me anymore. I want my body back—my whole body. I want me back.*

On the TV, Clint Eastwood sat in a covered wagon with a couple of Native American children, singing a song to them on a guitar. The doctor had set the TV to a channel devoted to old shows from the 1950s and 60s: *Rawhide, I Dream of Jeannie, I Love Lucy, Bewitched* and *The Andy Griffith Show*. The schedule for the day was displayed between programs, and Peter was finally able to tell time because of it. *Rawhide* was on, which meant that it was a little past nine o' clock in the morning.

At one point a commercial came on announcing that *True Grit* would be playing on the channel "this Sunday, June sixteenth".

It's June, he thought with grim dismay. *My last memories are from December. Six months of my life are gone. I've been trapped here for half a year.*

It wasn't until *The Honeymooners* came on at five o' clock in the evening did the door finally open again. More light crept into the room. Standing in the doorway was the dark shape of the doctor.

"Peter," he said.

Peter turned his head away and shut his eyes, ignoring the pain in his neck. He couldn't look at this man. The sight of him was offensive. He clenched his fists—the one that was his own, and the other that wasn't.

Footsteps approached his bed, and he heard the legs of the doctor's chair drag against the floor as he sat down.

"Peter, I have food for you."

Peter didn't respond, didn't even open his eyes. He was so hungry. His insides felt hollow, and his stomach cried out for him to accept the food, but he couldn't.

"I heard you, Peter," Jacob said bluntly. His voice was faint. "Last night, I heard you screaming."

Shut up, shut up. Peter clenched his teeth. *Just leave me alone.*

"You're probably feeling a lot of things," he went on. "This… is to be expected. You are traumatized, confused, angry and depressed. It was foolish of me to think… that when you did regain your strength, you wouldn't understand. I guess I just didn't see things that far until now."

Leave me alone. Just GO!

"I'm sorry, Peter. For everything. I think I've made a mistake. I'll leave the food here, whenever you wish to eat."

The chair slid against the floor again, Jacob's footsteps walked out, and the door shut firmly. Peter opened his eyes and stared at the ceiling.

That spider was there still, barely visible in the glow of the television, but Peter could see it. Its web was complete, and it rested near the middle. The credits for *The Honeymooners* rolled and *Bewitched* came on.

Peter thought of his family, of Jack, Erin, Margie and his brother Owen. The thought of them motivated him to escape. He needed to make sure that they were safe. The doctor clearly wasn't telling him everything. If something had happened to him, then had anything happened to them? What was this gut feeling he kept getting whenever he thought of Jack?

Soon, when I'm sure the time is right.

Given the condition of his body, Peter figured that he may not be strong enough to escape just yet, but he would need to come up with a plan—at the very least, case the joint.

11.

An episode of *Annie Oakley* came on at nine o' clock the following morning. Besides the TV, it was quiet. The pipes didn't creak, footsteps didn't tap overhead, nor was there any music.

Peter was certain that the doctor would have come in by now. He usually fed Peter either a bowl of broth or baby food in the morning—never more, never less. When Peter once complained, the doctor had insisted: "Your body can't handle anything more than this." After eating, he would give Peter his medications and shots, then leave.

The Beverly Hillbillies came on at eleven. The doctor still hadn't come in, nor was any noise heard around the house. *Where is he?* Peter thought. *Something's not right.*

What the doctor had told him haunted him: "*I'm sorry, Peter. For everything. I think I've made a mistake.*"

What did he mean by this? Was he losing his grip on himself? That was the last thing Peter needed. He was a prisoner in some hellhole, with the police looking for him, parts of his body removed or replaced, and now his only caregiver and sole means of human interaction was becoming threatening.

I'm living in an absurd comedy.

At five o' clock *The Munsters* came on. Fred Gwynne, done up in makeup and prosthetics to make him resemble a Karloff monster, sat at the Munster family table with a handkerchief tucked neatly into the front of his shirt. The Munster patriarch lectured his wolf-son that how you looked on the outside didn't matter, as long as your heart was in the right place.

If there was a time for Peter to begin his plan, it was now. The spider above him had managed to snag a fly in its web. The fly jittered and flapped its wings but was unable to escape. The spider circled it, wrapping it up in a protein sarcophagus.

Do it.

Peter took a deep breath and tossed the sheet off himself. Looking at his body was something that he resented doing, but he kept Margie, Erin, and Jack firmly in the front of his mind. Peter took the bandages off his new, feminine hand and threw them away, then ran his fingers along his pasty skin, passing each rib until they clutched onto the tube attached to his chest.

Is this keeping me alive? If I pull it out, will it kill me?

You'll suffer something worse than death anyway if you don't pull it out. Just do it.

Peter turned the tube. His skin twisted around it. *Get it over with, like ripping off a band aid.* The skin pulled with the tube, and then it came off with a distinctive *pop* sound.

A long needle was attached to the end of the tube, dark red and dripping with blood. A throbbing sting emerged inside his chest. Blood ran from the small hole between his ribs, but it wasn't too much. He dropped the tube to the floor, popped off the second tube attached to his abdomen, then wiped up whatever blood there was using the bandages on his hand.

Just like the little engine in the story. I think I can, I think I can.

Peter rolled off the bed. The floor met him with a hard greeting. His new leg was still numb, and it was difficult to move it. On his hands and his right knee, Peter dragged himself over to the steel door. The knob did not resist when he reached up and grabbed it. Perhaps the doctor didn't lock it because he believed that Peter wouldn't remove the tubes attached to his torso, or even have the strength to get out of bed. Nonetheless, the door opened.

A decrepit cellar lay beyond. The concrete walls were stained from age and weather, flies danced around the bright fluorescent lights on the ceiling, and a putrid stench permeated the room. A wooden staircase along the right wall lead up to darkness. Steel tables were set up, but Peter was at too low an angle to see what was on them. A blackboard with mathematical equations covering it stood nearby.

There was a fold out chair near one of the tables. Peter crawled to it, dragging the new foot behind him as he went. He grabbed the seat of the chair and pulled himself up onto it.

On the table a human arm was propped up on some sort of contraption, hanging from where it was bolted by the exposed red head of its humerus. The flesh was badly bloated, and its veins bulged from its pale skin like purple roots. Wires were attached to it, running from the bend of the arm and the veins in the wrist to a large machine with dials on it.

"Oh Jesus, what the fuck is this?"

The arm repulsed Peter, especially the aroma of chemicals and human rot, but it morbidly arrested him as well. It was like his mind could not believe that what he was looking at was real. It had to have been a prop or something. Peter inched his index finger towards the arm and poked it. The arm twitched, then went limp.

"Shit! Fuck!" Peter yelped and fell backwards against a white steel box behind him. *This can't be real. This can't, this CAN'T—*

The steel box he landed on was a freezer. The cool air stung Peter's arms and hands, and the motor purred quietly. He turned around to face the freezer. *For the love of God, what is this nightmare place? Where is my family? Please, please tell me they're OKAY! Please tell me that this sick bastard didn't lay a finger on them.*

What if—?

In a fit of mania, Peter propped himself on his knee and opened the freezer. The pale eyes of a decapitated head stared up at him, her face expressionless and covered in frost. A human thigh rested against her cheek, along with a partially decomposed male torso.

Then he saw it. Lying atop the pile, the fingers perversely caressing the decapitated woman's hair, was his left hand. He recognized it by the scar on the knuckles from when Jeremy Hightower accidentally slid on it with his skate after Peter fell during a hockey game when he was sixteen.

Dully, Peter could hear ringing in his ears. His eyes rolled into the back of his head, and he tumbled over to the floor, fainting.

12.

When Peter came to, he was back in bed. The shape of the doctor sat hunched over by his feet on the mattress. Peter heard him sniffle, and the doctor's hands trembled anxiously between his knees.

Maybe it was empathy, or pure negligence, or both, but Peter whispered: "Jacob?"

The doctor looked at him. That youthful face was red and puffy. "Peter. You're awake."

Instinctively, Peter pulled himself up on his elbows.

"You got out. You've disconnected yourself from"—he gestured to the machine next to the bed—"that. You've been in my work area. Truth be told, I was sort of hoping you would see it for yourself." The doctor's face became frighteningly expressionless. "What did you think?"

"What kind of question is that? What did you do to me? No bullshit. Tell me!"

The doctor just stared at him.

"Where are my wife and children? I swear, if you've done anything to them, I'll kill you!"

"Your family is nowhere near here. They don't even know you're here."

"Then let me go. Jacob, please just let me go. I can't take this any longer."

"I made a mistake, Peter." Jacob's eyes were glassy and filled with pain. He pulled a syringe from his coat and took the cap off the needle. The vial was dense with some unknown chemical. "I'm sorry."

He's putting me down. The words flashed through Peter's mind. *Just like a sick pup—he's GOING TO KILL ME.*

Jacob stood. "I have more medicine for you."

"No."

"It's just something for your strength."

"No!"

The doctor lunged at him. Peter raised his arms and managed to press an elbow against his assailant's chest, keeping him at bay. His new hand reached up and grabbed the doctor's wrist, keeping it from coming down with the syringe.

The doctor's eyes widened and looked almost comical through the lenses of his thick glasses. He had clearly underestimated Peter's strength. "Peter!" he grunted. "Please, it's better this way. You have to believe me."

"Get off me, you mother fucker!"

"This is my mistake! Do you understand? You shouldn't be here!"

The doctor pushed all his weight down, and his face was only an inch away from Peter's. His terrified and grief-stricken eyes glared deep into Peter's. The arm was coming down, bringing that syringe closer.

Peter seized the opportunity. Weeks of pent-up rage came out. He lifted his head up and bit the doctor's nose.

The syringe fell and rolled off the bed to the floor. Peter grabbed the sides of the doctor's head, his teeth firmly gripped on his nose. The coppery taste of blood filled his mouth.

"Mother—fucker!"

"Peter! Stop!"

Jacob grabbed Peter by the hair and tried to pry him off. In that moment, Peter yanked his head back. The doctor fell backwards grabbing his face, and he tumbled over the TV. The TV smashed to the floor and shards of its screen scattered everywhere.

Peter rolled off the bed to the floor and struggled to his feet. His new leg was still limp, and his right leg trembled under his weight, but he managed to stand and hop to the door.

A hand swiped at his boxers. The doctor was on his knees. Blood dripped off his face against the front of his coat. He was trying to grab Peter.

Without thinking, Peter grabbed the doorknob for stability, then swung his new limp leg around and kicked the doctor in the face. Jacob flew back and landed on his back.

Peter yanked the door open, passed through that awful cellar operating room, and went up the wooden stairs.

"Peter!" Jacob cried. "Don't go!"

Peter ignored his calls, latched onto the railing and pulled himself up, hopping on one foot while his limp foot helplessly banged against each step he ascended. The door at the top was open, and Peter staggered through, finally leaving the cellar.

A moose head hung over a brick fireplace. Tacky blue wallpaper covered the walls, whereupon old, framed paintings of mountains and trains hung. A glass cabinet filled with carved stone animals sat in one corner of the room, and wooden furniture with dark brown cushions lay before a large bookcase.

This was not some secret underground laboratory, nor a government installation in the desert. It wasn't even a hospital. This looked like some sort of country house, a place for family vacations or romantic getaways. The banality of it left Peter astonished.

Grunts echoed up the staircase. Peter slammed the wooden door to the stairs shut and limped across the room to a screen door. *I'm almost out I'm almost out I NEED TO GET AWAY.* He barged through the screen door and out onto a porch with a couple of rocking chairs set up in front of the wooden railing. Peter resumed his escape, stumbling down the front steps and into the grass.

A forest surrounded him. It seemed to be the early hours of the morning. He looked over his shoulder as he fled to see what had been his prison all this time. It was a little nondescript single-story cabin in the woods, not unlike many in the country. A black flatbed truck was parked beside it under a tarp strung up by the branches of overhanging trees, and next to the truck was a white Toyota Corolla.

Peter ran through the woods. Sweat poured down his face. Every muscle screamed at him to slow down, but his terror fueled him to keep his ruined body going. Eventually, his body gave up and he fell flat on his face.

"Peter!" Jacob cried.

Gritting his teeth, Peter crawled away into a ditch filled with leaves. There was an overturned tree nearby, and its roots were exposed and strung with moldy clods of earth. Peter slipped under those roots, staring at the darkening sky.

"Don't do this to yourself!"

Peter pressed his new hand against his mouth, the skin cold and smooth. There was no way to pinpoint exactly where the doctor was, but judging by the sound of his voice, he was only a few yards away.

"You'll never come back from this, Peter!" Jacob shouted. He made a sound like spitting—probably blood. "You aren't meant for this world! There is nothing for you out there, Peter! Nothing!"

Once the echoes ceased, Peter didn't hear the doctor again. For a long time, he lay in that ditch, waiting. No sound. Nothing.

I'm free.

The whole world seemed to suddenly lift from his shoulders. A smile crept across his face for the first time in what felt like a lifetime.

Without realizing it, and having had no intention of doing so, the exhaustion overcame him. He fell asleep in that ditch, covered in dirt and leaves

Jayson Robert Ducharme

II.
LIFE

13.

A woodpecker's beak rattled against a tree. Another bird called out, singing. These sounds came to Peter, jarring him from sleep. He looked up at the bright blue summer sky. He wasn't aware of it, but it was June 18, a Tuesday—his first day of freedom.

Slowly, he crawled out of the ditch, stood, and then carefully balanced himself on his right leg. Once stable, he brushed the dirt off himself and out of his hair. Then, he took in a deep breath and exhaled. For the first time in too long, he couldn't smell human decomposition, chemicals, or musky cellar dust. This was air. It was fresh and hot, and it was sublime.

In every direction, he saw only trees. He knew that he would rather starve to death than ever go back to that cabin again. He needed to keep going and find something, anything.

Peter began his journey into the unknown.

14.

A little girl's voice: "I'll get you!"

Peter's head perked up. A sign of life—a young girl, no less. It was so beautiful to hear that Peter felt his throat swell. Then he remembered to not get too sentimental.

According to that doctor, I'm a wanted man. The police are looking for me. I don't know the extent to which I'm wanted, or how recognizable I will be to people. Keep your distance, Peter. Be selective about who you talk to.

Avoiding leaves and twigs, Peter followed the girl's voice.

"I got you now! You can't get away from me!"

A dog barked.

"Beth! Don't be so rough!" a woman called.

A house with dirty windows, chipping paint, and a rickety old back porch stood a few yards ahead in a clearing. A little girl, probably no more than ten years old, rolled around in the grass with a young Doberman. Standing nearby was a tired looking woman with her hair up in a messy bun—the girl's mother, Peter assumed. A laundry line stretched from the back porch to a tree, and the woman was clipping damp clothes to the line as she smoked a cigarette.

"Beth! What did I just say?"

"We ain't being rough!" The dog rubbed its snout into the girl's hair and sniffed aggressively. "When will Dad be home?"

"Later tonight." The woman clipped a T-shirt up, took the cigarette from her mouth and snapped it away. "Now come in. I need help with the dishes. Ferdinand is gonna need a bath anyway. Come on! *Allons! Se depecher!*"

The girl and dog trotted up the porch and followed the mother into the house through a sliding glass door. Once the door clapped shut in its frame, the coast seemed clear.

Peter swallowed and looked down at his ruined body. If the cops were after him, the worst thing he could do was go around looking the way he did now. He squinted at the clothesline. Blouses, a little girl's dress, some socks, and a large flannel shirt with jeans hung from the line, swaying to and fro in the breeze.

Just go.

Peter crept out from behind a tree, then hopped through the yard as fast as he could, moving himself forward on his good leg while trying to use the other for balance and support. He went for the flannel and jeans, and he yanked them off the line as he passed, hearing the clips snap off.

The dog's muffled barking erupted in the house.

"Fuck!" Peter pressed the clothes to his chest and fled back to the woods. He struggled up a narrow slope, fell, and then crawled the rest of the way with his elbow and knee. Once up the slope, he scrambled back to his feet and escaped into the trees.

The slider opened. The barks grew louder. "What the hell is it, dog?" the woman shouted.

Keep pushing! Peter imagined that animal chasing him. Keeping his eyes forward, he spotted the ditch he had fallen asleep in. Peter flew into the ditch and took cover. In the distance, the barks echoed, but then it all went quiet again.

Peter crawled out of the ditch and held up his new clothes. A red and black flannel shirt dotted with little holes that looked to have been made by neglected cigarettes. There was some grime on the jeans—perhaps someone in the family was a machinist or worked on cars.

The flannel fit well enough, but the pants were baggy around his waist and slacked over his feet. Peter wasn't sure if this was because he had lost so much weight or if the owner of the jeans was a large person. Regardless, he rolled the waistline of the pants until they fit, and the pant legs rose above his ankles. He took a moment to examine his feet. His own foot wiggled its toes. The big toe of his new foot moved, but none of the others did. It wasn't much, but it was progress.

15.

In the distance Peter heard the familiar sound of a highway—cars zooming at high speeds, carrying gusts of turbulence behind them. Peter picked up the pace. A two-lane interstate appeared beyond the trees. From where Peter stood, he couldn't see any signs.

Near the highway, only a short walk away, he saw a hamlet. A main road lined with telephone poles cut through a little town with wooden and brick buildings. Red, white and blue flags with "OPEN" stitched into the white strips hung outside quaint log cabin inns, mom and pop shops, and gas stations. Surrounding the town, a never-ending landscape of bright green mountains rose and fell for miles.

Peter descended from the forest to the town.

The main road was barren save for a couple of cars parked on the curb. "LIVE FREE OR DIE" the license plates declared.

I'm in New Hampshire, Peter thought with some relief. *I'm not thousands of miles away from home, but still far enough away for it to be a problem. My home in Atkinson is about a two-hour drive from the mountains. The interstate I saw must be I-89 or I-93. Depending on which, if I just move south, I can get home.*

For several moments he debated on whether or not to go into the old shanty gas station, the building nearest to him. It was a sad looking shack with two rusty pumps under an overarching roof. Ancient signs for beers hung in the dusty windows, and an overflowing trash bin surrounded by cigarette butts sat next to one of the pumps. Slipping his feminine hand into his pocket, Peter pulled the door open and stepped in.

Only two shelves with canned soups, engine oil and bags of coffee on them lined the back of the gas station. A balding old man sat on a stool reading the paper behind the register. The man's dirty hands left black smears on the edges of the pages.

"Excuse me," Peter said.

The man brought the paper down. The moment he saw Peter, his eyes opened for several moments, then relaxed. "Can I help you?"

"I'm a little lost."

The man set the paper on the counter and his eyes scanned Peter head to toe. Awkwardly, Peter tried to hide his new foot behind his leg. The man raised an eyebrow at this gesture. "How lost?"

"What town am I in?"

"You're in Woodstock."

"Woodstock?"

"That's what I said."

Woodstock was a little town in the White Mountains. Peter knew about it because Owen used to go fishing in Lincoln, a town right nearby. Woodstock meant that the interstate Peter had seen was, in fact, I-93. This was good because it was a direct way home from the mountains. Yet, if the police were after him, then how was he supposed to get to Atkinson? There were no buses or trains that ran out of Woodstock, as far as he knew—not like he had any money anyway.

"Sir," the man said, pressing his hands flat against the countertop, "are you some sort of vet?"

"Excuse me?"

"Lots of vets coming back from the desert homeless, especially since they started pulling boys out of Afghanistan."

"I'm not a veteran."

"I see. I just thought maybe you were. I get vets coming in here without homes sometimes."

"Why would you think I served?"

"On account of your face, mister. Like you were wounded."

A burning terror ignited in Peter's stomach. He raised his hand and caressed one side of his face with his fingertips.

"You good?"

"No," Peter said faintly, turning to the door. "Thank you for your time."

Peter returned to the forest. For several minutes, he sat against a tree with his knees up and his arms resting on top of them. A small, murky swamp lay a few meters away to his right.

My face. Something is wrong with my face.

He lifted his left hand up. When his mind commanded it to move, it obediently did so. The fingers curled and spread. This hand belonged to someone else—a woman—and yet he could control it. He pressed his palms together, and he could immediately sense the feminine touch of his left hand against his right. The touch reminded him of his wife and daughter.

The idea came to him to look into the waters of the swamp. It looked deep enough to see his own vague reflection. The idea was terrible, but it was more tormenting to not look and let his imagination go wild.

Slowly, he stood and lumbered toward the swamp and stood on a mossy rock. Tadpoles swam around beneath that dirty water. He clenched his fists, moved himself forward, and spotted the shape of himself in the water—

—then he recoiled. *No, I can't.* He stepped away and covered his eyes with his hands. *I am Peter Murphy. This is MY BODY. There are parts of me that have been replaced. No different from an organ or limb transplant. Just because somebody gets a new hand or leg doesn't suddenly make them not themselves anymore. I'm still Peter Murphy, god damn it. I'M STILL ME.*

Then why are you so scared to look at yourself?

Peter paced back and forth, gently clapping his hands together—a nervous habit that he had adopted from his mother—trying to think of what to do.

Once he returned to Atkinson and reunited with his family, then he could figure out what had happened to him and why the police were after him. Until then, he didn't feel safe going to the authorities. What crime did he commit? How serious was it? He doubted Jacob would have warned him ahead of time if it wasn't serious. *I'm not a murderer, am I?*

If he was truly guilty of something serious, then he was willing to turn himself in. He didn't think that he could live a normal life knowing that he had done something horrible, even if he did survive his current bizarre predicament. Until then, he needed to see his family. He needed to know that they were okay. That was his priority. Dealing with the police could come after that.

Yet, how could he get to Atkinson? He had no money, no car, nothing. It would take days to walk down the interstate and doing that would be begging a state trooper to see him.

An idea came to him, but it was one that he didn't like. Given his circumstances though, he didn't think he had a choice.

Once he felt comfortable enough, he followed his tracks through the woods.

16.

Nightfall. Katydids sang, and an owl hooted somewhere far off, unseen. The forest was pitch black, which made it easier to spot the cabin he had escaped from. Its windows glowed yellow like a pair of eyes. Peter knelt behind a tree about twenty yards away, surveying it, filled with dread and rage.

He held a thick, long stick. If he saw that doctor, it would be difficult for him to not attack him mercilessly for what he did to him. Peter felt nothing but utter contempt for Jacob Abbot.

The black flatbed truck was still parked next to the cabin, precisely where he had seen it as he escaped. Next to the truck was the Toyota, covered in sap and pine needles, its white paint stained with dirt and grime from the elements. It looked like the truck had seen more recent use than the Toyota.

Would the doctor call the police?

No, he wouldn't. Why would he? He had been keeping a hostage who was possibly a fugitive from justice. Not to mention all the god-awful shit in the cellar. Calling the cops would mean bringing the cops to him too.

For at least a half hour, Peter squatted waiting and watching; at no point did he see any shadows pass the windows. He heard no music or other sounds. He rolled the stick between his hands, nervous and impatient.

It's been long enough.

Peter approached the house. His feminine hand reached out and grabbed the knob of the screen door. The moment he opened it and crossed the threshold, the stench hit him. Having been freed of the basement and experienced fresh air again, the smell of this place became insufferable.

The door leading to the basement was open. Beyond the doorway lay darkness and Peter could hear water dripping within.

Make this quick.

The key rack next to the front door was empty. *Where the fuck are the keys?* He tip-toed across the room and entered the kitchen. Pine cabinets hung over an iron stove and an old sink filled with neglected dishes covered in mold. No keys were on the table.

Come on, where are they?

Peter approached a door to his right. The moment he opened it, he saw the visage of someone directly ahead of him and, in a panic, he flung the stick at it wildly.

The stick snapped on impact, and then glass shattered. Shards rained against a porcelain sink and the tiled floor. The empty, wooden frame of a ruined mirror hung across from where Peter stood in the bathroom.

Peter froze, afraid to move, staring stupidly at the mess he had made. He quickly slipped out of the bathroom and shut the door, afraid to catch a glimpse of himself in one of those broken shards.

Something began moving beneath the floor. The sound of light footfalls whispered against those concrete walls below.

They quietly echoed up the stairs and through the doorway to the basement.

Panic took hold. Peter stepped out of the bathroom and rushed through the kitchen back in the living room. As if by providence, his eyes caught sight of a brown jacket slung across an arm of the couch next to the front door. He flew to the coat and snatched it up, checking one pocket, then another.

Come on, come on—

Keys jingled in the breast pocket. Peter fingered them out, savoring their weight in his palm.

Those footfalls ascended the stairs. Somebody stood within the darkness beyond the basement doorway.

Clutching the keys, Peter fled the cabin for the second time, and then circled around to the truck and Toyota. He yanked open the driver door of the Toyota first, slipped behind the wheel, then jabbed the keys into the ignition. They wouldn't fit.

"Shit!"

Peter kicked the driver door open, stumbled out, then got into the truck. It took him three tries, but he managed to get the keys into the ignition. They fit and he turned them.

Please have gas please have gas please have gas.

The dashboard lit up and the headlights shined against the trees ahead. The gas needle rose and settled a little past the halfway point. *Good enough.*

Peter fiddled with the stick, then rolled the truck out from beneath the tarp, and drove it—carefully and yet urgently—away from the cabin and through the woods. He followed torn up grass and muddy old tire tracks. That godforsaken cabin sank away in the rearview mirror behind him, and then it was gone.

17.

Peter couldn't see the sun itself, but its emerging presence slowly took the night away. The mountains became visible, and as Peter made his way down the interstate, he could see hints of civilization. The occasional far-off house in the landscape appeared, and town names became more familiar with each exit he passed. Sometimes he saw construction workers, surrounded by orange cones and wearing bright yellow vests, tearing up the pavement with jackhammers.

Just past Exit 10 was a large visitor center near Hooksett for people traveling to the more touristy destinations of the state. A long line of gas pumps dotted the middle of the spacious parking lot next to the visitor center, which featured a general store, several grab-n-go restaurants, and a few information booths.

Peter was thankful that the visitor center was mostly empty. He needed to stop and think for a little while, so he pulled in and settled towards the back of the lot. Only a few cars were parked in front of the center—employees, he figured—and someone was pumping gas in her van. For a long time, Peter sat in his stolen vehicle, hands on the wheel, terrified.

The closer he got to Atkinson, the more frighteningly real all this became. To some degree, he had tried to rationalize everything that had happened to him up to that point—the kidnapping, the mutilation of his body, the police, everything. He compartmentalized these things while he focused on staying alive and escaping. Now that he was as close to home as he was, apprehension consumed him. The answers to all his questions seemed overwhelming to consider.

What if the police wanted him because of something he had done to his loved ones? *Am I capable of such a thing?* It seemed impossible to him, but a lot of things had seemed impossible by this point. What if he went home and found something worse than anything he'd experienced up to now?

I just want everything to be normal again. None of this needed to happen… I just want to go home. I want to be with my children and my wife. Why is that so scary?

In the driver's side mirror, Peter spotted a state trooper's cruiser pulling into the visitor center—those familiar, dark brown and green Dodge Chargers with the emblem of the Old Man on the Mountain on the doors. The trooper parked in front of the visitor center, got out and went inside.

Peter started the truck up and pulled back onto the interstate. As he drove, he was very careful to avoid looking into the rearview mirror. He was still petrified to even catch a glimpse of himself.

18.

The rest of the trip down, besides some traffic, was no problem. It took only a little less than an hour to get to Atkinson from the visitor center. Once he got to Exit 3, he pulled off and took NH-111 directly into town.

Peter turned onto Argyle Road. This was his street. Lining the street were meek houses with large stone stoops, wooden porches, gardens, and above ground pools surrounded by plastic white fences. The Dalton kids, twelve and thirteen, were running around their yard spraying each other with squirt guns. A couple walked their big yellow Labrador, and toddlers wearing colorful helmets rode around on tricycles. Yellow pollen powdered the pavement and there wasn't a cloud in the sky. It was an average early summer day.

Everything felt so normal. For the first time since he had escaped, Peter felt—if just momentarily—calm. He even felt a little excited. It was as if the neighborhood was telling him that everything was going to be okay.

There it was. His house sat near the intersection where Argyle met Wollstone Avenue. It was a yellow house with white window shutters. On the front lawn, Margie's garden was empty. Margie always began her gardening at the end of April, and it usually blossomed around this time in June, with big winding plants and purple flowers. Now it was a barren mulch patch.

Only one vehicle was parked in the driveway, Margie's white van. Peter's dark green Chevrolet was nowhere to be seen. Peter pulled the truck up next to the van, killed the engine and got out.

The front door was locked. *Right, I forgot.* He pulled back the welcome mat and plucked the spare key out from beneath, then unlocked the door and burst into the house.

"Kids! Margie!"

A massive grin spread across his face and his eyes glassed over. The living room was left just as he had remembered it. A black leather couch sat across from a large flat screen TV with game consoles lying comfortably on the carpet. Margie's enlarged and framed photographs of Mexican architecture were still hanging on the walls; she had taken the photos herself on a trip that she, Peter and Erin went on to New Mexico a few months before Jack was born.

"Kids? Kids, it's me! It's Dad!"

Peter stomped up the hallway to the bedrooms. The first door he went to was Erin's and he barged in. The room was empty. Erin's paintings of lions and wolves were no longer hanging on the walls. Some of her art books sat on the bureau, and her bed was neatly folded, the pillows devoid of compression. It looked like nobody had slept in it for a long time.

"Erin?" he whispered. *Where's your art? Where's your easel?*

Peter crossed his daughter's room and opened the closet. Most of her clothes were gone, save for a few dresses and coats. Her easel was folded up against the back of the closet, along with an unfinished portrait of an orange cat. The cat painting was the same one that she had begun work on back in December.

"What is this?"

Peter stepped out and crossed the hall to his son's room. Jack's army man blankets and comforter were gone, and his bed mattress sat bare on its frame. His toy dinosaurs and plastic forts, which usually littered the floor, were nowhere to be seen.

Several cardboard boxes were stacked in the corner. Peter pulled open the top flap of one of the boxes and found his son's stuffed animal fox and plastic race cars. The beady black eyes of the fox peered up at him, as if hopeful for adoption.

Everything Peter found in his house only fueled his worst suspicions. He backed out of Jack's room and shut the door. The final door at the end of the hall beckoned him.

"Margie?" he croaked.

Peter stepped into the bedroom he shared with Margie. The bed was a mess, and Margie's dirty laundry was all over the floor. The closet door was opened, and the body mirror that Margie always used to survey what she was going to wear for the day hung on it. The bureau, where the framed family photos always were, was cleared. No more pictures of Erin dressed as a cat and Jack as a pirate for Halloween, or of Peter and Margie's wedding, or of Owen playing with the kids. In place of the pictures were dozens of cards.

Peter picked up one of the cards. A drawing of a bundle of roses was on the front. "OUR CONDOLENCES" it read. On the inside someone had written, "Margie, I have no words. Know that our hearts are always open to you. The world won't be the same without Peter and Jack. Call us."

It was signed by Margie's co-workers. From what he could see, the rest of the cards on the bureau were sympathy cards as well. Among them was a pot of long dead lilies with a tag in the soil that read: "IN OUR THOUGHTS".

Someone was breathing behind him. Peter dropped the card and turned around. In the doorway, Margie stood. Her face was pasty and her eyes were dark and red. Her hair was stringy, and her clothes—a sleeveless casual blouse and jeans—were covered in stains. It looked like she hadn't slept or washed in days and had lost a considerable amount of weight.

"Margie." Peter approached her, unable to think of what to say. He didn't understand anything he was seeing.

This ghostly visage of his wife glared at him. Her eyes widened. Briefly, her mouth opened, and she pressed her fingertips against her lips.

"Margie, I'm here. I'm alive."

In a flash, a look of unrestrained desire crossed her face, but then it was gone. Her brow furrowed, and a deep pain emerged from her eyes. Her hand fell away from her lips and pressed against Peter's cheek.

"Where are the kids, Margie? What happened?"

Margie grimaced and pulled her hand away. Then she took a step back.

"Wait, Margie."

"No."

"What's—"

"No!"

Her lips peeled back, barring her teeth, and her hands clawed at her hair. She began hyperventilating.

"Margie, it's me!" He put his hands on her. "What's wrong?"

"Don't touch me!" She shoved him. Her voice rose to a shrill, anguished cry. "Get away from me!"

"I came back, baby. I'm here!"

"Get away from me!" She yanked large tufts of hair out of her scalp and screamed. Tears poured down her face, and then she fled.

"Wait!"

"Stay away!"

She ran down the hall. Peter did not chase her. He stood in the bedroom, listening to the front door open and slam shut. The van outside started up, and Peter heard its tires screeching against the pavement as she pulled out of the driveway and sped down the street. The roar of the engine passed by the house, and then faded into silence.

That was when he saw the monster.

Its eyes were different colors—one bright blue, the other dark brown. It looked like some deformed beast wearing a mask that resembled Peter Murphy. It had his eyebrows, lips, and nose, but the structure beneath was disjoined, like it didn't fit. The skin was leathery and drooped under the eyeballs, and the red tissue in the sockets could be seen. The creature pulled its lips back, and its filthy green teeth were exposed.

Peter took a step towards the monster. The monster took a step towards him. Peter reached out to touch the monster. The monster reached out to touch him. Peter's fingertips pressed against the cold glass of the body mirror on the closet door.

"No."

The monster mouthed "No" back.

This can't be me. This isn't—THIS CANNOT BE ME!

Peter drove his fists into the mirror. The glass shattered, cutting his knuckles, and shards cluttered to the floor. He grabbed his face and began pulling on the flesh attached to his skull. "It's not me! *IT'S NOT ME! IT'S NOT! IT'S NOT!*"

He started choking and gagging, and he fell to his hands and knees, feeling his insides retch and twist. And then he screamed. It came out in labored howls like an animal.

"This isn't me!" he kept sobbing.

But it was.

19.

For hours, Peter lay in the empty bathtub with the curtain shut. The walls of the tub were smeared in his bright red blood from the cuts in his knuckles that he had gotten when he smashed the mirror. He didn't care.

The ruin that had once been his life surrounded him. After seeing himself in the mirror, he had gone on a rampage through the house. He had ripped apart his bedroom, knocking over furniture and tearing the sheets off the bed. He had yanked the fan out of the ceiling in the living room and pitched it at the TV. He had opened all the cabinets in the kitchen and flung everything inside out. He had thrown boxes of cereal, glass jars of jelly, and cans of soup to the floor in a massive concoction of broken glass and food. The cuts on his hands had smeared everything he touched with blood.

The rampage had only stopped when he had seen something stuck to the refrigerator with a magnet. It was a newspaper clipping: "PETER KIERAN (37) AND JOHN PATRICK 'JACK' MURPHY (2)".

Peter had clawed the obituary off the fridge and read it over several times. Eventually he fell to the floor in a sitting position with the article resting against his lap.

It read: *Peter and Jack Murphy, both of Atkinson, passed away unexpectedly in Haverhill on Sunday, December 22. Peter was the beloved husband of Marjorie (Strauss) Murphy for twelve years, and Jack was the couple's lively and imaginative son. Jack had an older sister, Erin, who loved him very much. Jack was an active boy who loved dinosaurs and playing with his army men. Peter was passionate about academia, and personally believed that the world could be a better place with more access to education. Memorial services will be held at the O'Tool and Craft Funeral Home in Atkinson on Saturday, January 4. Funeral services will follow the next morning at 8 a.m. in Atkinson Cemetery.*

The Modern Prometheus

The photos in the obituary were Peter's staff portrait and a picture of Jack pushing around a plastic toy lawnmower in the backyard, the kind that blew out bubbles as you pushed it.

A tear had landed against the obituary by the time he finished reading. Peter pressed it against his chest, then got up and mournfully retreated to the bathroom. That had been when he climbed into the bathtub and shut the curtain.

My son and I are dead, he kept thinking. *But why am I here? Why?*

Was there some kind of misunderstanding? Was his body buried in Atkinson Cemetery and he was now just some kind of specter? What was the doctor doing with him? How had he and Jack died, and furthermore, why was he still here and not Jack? Where was Erin, and was she safe?

Many of these questions seemed superfluous, given what he had discovered, along with the implications behind it all. The only thing that seemed to matter was the crushing realization that *he wasn't supposed to be here.*

Dark orange sunlight crept across the bathroom as evening approached. Peter decided to finally get out of the tub. Carefully, he slipped the obituary into his pocket, and then pulled himself out. He went to the medicine cabinet and wrapped his bleeding hands up in gauze, then stepped out of the bathroom and went to the hall closet.

A small step ladder leaned against the back of the closet behind boxes of Halloween and Christmas decorations. Peter pulled the ladder out, unfolded it, and then stepped up to reach the top shelf. He pulled out a rectangular plastic case, stepped down and stood with his back pressed against the wall.

Peter wiped dust off the top of the case. Up until now, he had no reason to ever take this case out from its hiding place. Licking his lips, he undid the latches and opened it. Within, a pistol and magazine lay neatly tucked into foam. The magazine, he knew, was already loaded.

A few months before Jack was born, Owen's duplex had gotten robbed. Thankfully, Owen hadn't been home at the time, but his TV, air conditioner, and numerous electronics were stolen. It looked like the burglars had broken the kitchen window open to get in. With a new baby on the way, Peter got paranoid.

Margie had been outraged when Peter brought the firearm home. "I don't want this shit around the house! This isn't Lowell!" were her exact words. After a few weeks, Margie stopped heckling Peter over it, despite her disapproval. She had instructed him to keep it on the top shelf of the closet, out of reach of the children, and to never tell anyone that he had bought it.

The Modern Prometheus

For two and a half years, this gun sat in its case, hidden in the closet. Peter ran his fingertips along the steel, sensing its power. He closed the case and tucked it under his arm. He had resigned himself to his circumstances and stepped outside.

The neighborhood was clearing out, save for a few teenagers down the street bouncing a basketball around. The world had been oblivious to Peter's outburst and Margie's escape. All the better.

The van was gone. There were skid marks on the pavement from when Margie peeled out of the driveway. If she had gone to the police, they would have been here by now. That meant she had gone elsewhere, and Peter already had a theory as to where.

Doesn't matter. It's getting dark out. Better make this quick.

He descended the stoop, got into the truck, and drove away.

20.

Atkinson Cemetery was at the edge of town, near the Massachusetts border. Peter knew where it was. It was the same cemetery his mother was buried in, and he didn't imagine either himself or Jack would be far from her.

It wasn't a fancy cemetery. A meek rock wall surrounded the property, and there was a single gated entrance where a road went in from the street. A little white sign with black painted letters that read "ATKINSON CEMETERY" hung next to the entrance.

By the time Peter arrived and parked the truck on the side of the street, night had fallen. He entered the cemetery and followed a path through the rolling hills of the property, passing headstones bearing the names HENAULT and LEBREQUE and MILLER. Tombstones of all shapes and sizes surrounded him, and then he saw it: MURPHY.

His mother's headstone was a small granite rectangle protruding from the grass. "COLLEEN CHERYL MURPHY 1950 – 2014" was engraved in bold letters on it. Moss coated the headstone and the grass around it was overgrown. A couple of fake roses, weathered and stained, were tangled up in the grass. It looked like the same fake roses Peter and Owen had planted for Mother's Day the year before.

Directly next to his mother was another MURPHY headstone. A newer one, made of dark purple marble, and laminated freshly enough to make the names "JOHN PATRICK" and "PETER KIERAN" glimmer under the bright stars.

What was in front of him could not be denied. Peter fell to his knees before the headstone. *We're supposed to be buried together, Jack. We left the world together and we were supposed to cross that river together. Now you're all alone, under that soil.*

The Modern Prometheus

Peter pressed his face against his son's name. He tried to imagine Jack, his bright soft hair tickling his chin and cheek, or his warm baby skin. All he could feel was marble, hot from the summer heat. He thought about all the things he wanted his son to have. He fantasized about Jack getting his license, and surprising him with a new car; graduating high school, grabbing that diploma and looking out into the crowd at Peter smiling at him; going to college, getting married and having kids.

None of that was ever going to happen now. Whatever Jack's life had been in Peter's memories was all that he would ever be.

Peter pulled himself off the headstone and set the gun case in the grass. He took the gun and magazine out of the foam, eyed the bullets tucked in the follower, then slipped the magazine into the gun and pulled back on the slide, hearing the *click* of a bullet entering the chamber.

A world without you is not worth living.

Peter raised the gun and pressed the barrel against his forehead. He was scared, but he knew that he was an abomination of nature. To remain here would be an insult to the order of the universe. He needed to be with his child again.

Slowly, Peter's thumb began to squeeze the trigger.

A voice whispered in his mind: *Wait, Peter.*

His thumb stopped, leaving the trigger half pulled. He allowed his thumb to relax, and the gun fell into the grass at his knees. He found himself looking up at the stars, his mind blank.

What if...?

Unless...?

All sorts of thoughts came to him in that moment, just before his resignation to return to the salt finished what it had intended. Ringing sounded in his ears, and the stars seemed to swim in the black sky.

I understand it all so clearly now.

There was no real way of gauging just how long he knelt there, hypnotized by space. Eventually, he picked the gun up, tucked it into the front of his pants and got up. He drifted through and out of the cemetery like a phantom, his mind possessed.

A new purpose had come together in his heart. He felt that he may know why he had been brought back into this world. He just needed more information, a complete understanding of what had happened to him and his son. If he was still here because of what he suspected, then he would engage in what his heart now told him to do.

"Don't worry, Jack," Peter whispered to himself as he got back into the truck. "I'm gonna set all this right again."

21.

In the morning, Peter awoke on the floor of Jack's barren room. Against his chest he held Jack's stuffed animal fox. It brought him some comfort. One of its eyes was loose, and along the left paw was red stitching from when Mr. Fox needed an "operation" after Jack accidentally ripped him playing too hard. Margie had stitched it up nicely, and the boy had been none the wiser.

Peter got up, tucked Mr. Fox under his arm and groggily stepped into the living room. Through the window he could see that Margie's van still wasn't in the driveway. He sat down on the leather couch, observing the mess he had created during his rampage. He eyed the flipped over coffee table, the smashed TV, and the ruined ceiling fan lying on the floor in a heap.

A grumble emerged from his stomach. He was starving. Solemnly, Peter got up, went into the kitchen, opened the fridge and reviewed what was left inside, which was barely anything. A jug of milk, some sliced cheese and a few Greek yogurts. Peter took a few yogurts and grabbed a spoon off the floor.

As he ate, Peter theorized that his wife went to her mother Helena's house in Manchester. He also assumed that Erin was up there too. There had been a few occasions in their marriage where Margie needed to stay with her mother for a while. Once, when she had fallen into a serious depression following Jack's birth, and another time when she and Peter had gotten into a stupid argument over the house mortgage. Helena Strauss was always open to take her daughter and grandchildren in no matter what the situation was. In some ways Peter suspected that it even pleased Helena to do this in some passive-aggressive way.

One of the things that bonded Peter and Margie together was that neither had known their fathers and shared close relationships with their mothers.

When he was five years old, Peter's father left. There was no answer as to why, nor any clue as to where he went. The best guess Colleen Murphy had was that he went back to Ireland and got involved with the IRA. Whenever she read about a car bombing or shooting in Northern Ireland, Mom was terrified that the name "Finnegan Murphy" would appear. It never did, and what had happened to Dad became one of those great mysteries that Peter had to accept he would never solve.

Mom was Irish too, but third generation. Born in Lawrence, she had been the oldest of five sisters. She had forgone college and began working as a housekeeper at various hotels to support her family. She had Peter when she was about twenty years old, and Owen not long after. After dad left, Mom became a rugged lady. The Murphy family bounced around a lot when Peter and Owen were kids—moving from Lawrence to Newburyport, then to Somerville, before eventually settling in North Andover. They shared a tight apartment with almost no privacy, and oftentimes Peter and his brother were unsupervised because Mom was pulling long hours at the hotel. In the morning she worked as a housekeeper, and in the evenings she was a custodian at the same hotel. She'd get up at six in the morning and wouldn't be back until eleven at night—including weekends. When she would get home, she'd have a few beers, smoke on the balcony, then tuck Owen and Peter into bed together and kiss them goodnight. They only had two beds—one for the boys, and one for Mom.

She taught them to cook and clean for themselves. When they got too rough around the apartment, they always cleaned up after themselves, knowing that Mom would spank them hard enough for them to sleep on their stomachs for the night. If there was anything Peter was thankful for, it was that he had learned to be self-sufficient at a young age.

Once every few months, Mom managed to make valuable time with her children. She loved to take the boys to Canobie Lake Park. These few occasions were when she actually seemed happy. She'd plant herself comfortably between her children on the rides with her arms around them, her hands stinking of cigarettes and disinfectant. As they zipped around, she'd squeeze them tight and scream and laugh with them as they went up, down and around.

"A son of a bitching time!" she'd always exclaim as they got off. "I felt you two holding on to your Mama tight. Don't you boys worry. I've always got a hold on you."

Peter cherished the memories he had of his mother. Despite her absence, Peter knew that she had loved him and his brother. She had done everything she possibly could to ensure that they could have futures. Peter never had a chance to thank her for that before cervical cancer took her away. He always regretted that.

Thinking of his mother compelled him to meditate on his own family. He finished off the yogurts, pitched the empty cups and dirty spoons into the sink, and then went down the hall to the bedrooms. The door to the room he shared with Margie was still open. He stepped in, lamenting the disaster he had created. The sheets and comforter were torn off the bed, and the grieving cards were shredded and thrown about like confetti. The glass shards of the mirror littered the carpet.

I really lost myself, didn't I?

Given what had happened to him, he tried not to beat himself up about it too much.

What had become of his wife horrified him. She looked like some miserable shadow of her former self. He wished that he could hold her and take away her pain, but he knew that he couldn't.

They had met when Peter was twenty-three and Margie was twenty-one, as students at Southern New Hampshire University in Manchester. Peter had just begun his master's and Margie was on the tail end of her bachelor's in civil engineering. She had put off—to quote—"all those awful English classes" to her final few semesters because she couldn't stand them. Math and science were more her forte. Peter thought that math and science were a load of horseshit, and she thought that the humanities were horseshit, so neither had expected to get on as well as they had.

Margie had been assigned to Peter as her literature tutor, and they met twice a week at the library. Peter had sympathized with Margie's struggle, as she had been enrolled in Early American Literature and was up to her eyes in political and philosophical essays—a lot of Thoreau, Paine, and Franklin. Very dry.

Regardless of their differences, Margie had taken a liking to him. Peter had a way of "explaining things that brought clarity to dense, long-winded bullshit." Peter had been charmed. They started going to the movies and went fishing along the Merrimack River. If somebody had told Peter that this quiet girl—who delighted in lecturing him on theoretical physics just to watch the dumbfounded look on his face—would become the mother of his children, he'd have laughed off the whole thing. Yet, that was what ended up happening, and it was the best thing that had ever happened to him.

Margie's mother was a whole can of worms to deal with when they started dating. Put simply, Helena was ferocious when it came to protecting her daughter from men. Margie's father had been a deadbeat drunk with a gambling addiction, and she had spent the first few years of her life in a household where jewelry, electronics, and even the refrigerator were at risk of being gambled away.

When Margie was five years old, Reggie Strauss had drunkenly beaten a man nearly to death over his gambling debts in the backroom of a bar. The guy's face had been mutilated with a broken beer bottle. He had been arrested and charged with assault with a deadly weapon and attempted murder. Soon after that, Helena filed for divorce, then took her daughter and moved to an apartment in Manchester. Margie never saw her father again. Once, her father had written a letter to her, but Margie left it unopened and gave it to her mother, who burned it in the sink. After a few years, Helena managed to scrounge together enough money to buy a small house in the city to raise her daughter, and there she stayed.

The first time Peter ever met Helena Strauss was after about six months of dating Margie. Margie had taken him to see her mother because she felt that their relationship was getting serious, and she wanted her mother to know this. Margie had warned Peter again and again that her mother would not approve of him but would at the very least be civil. It wasn't something she wanted to do, but felt she had to get it over with.

Helena had answered the door and invited Peter and her daughter in. They got comfortable on the couch and Helena sat in the recliner across from them. She smiled at them politely, but her face was like stone, and her eyes were fixated on Peter, filled with animosity. Margie knew what her mother was doing and tried to ease the tension with casual conversation—about school, work, and the future.

Helena played into the light talk, nodding here and there, going "Mhm" to certain things, and sometimes pitched an anecdote in for good humor. All the while though, her glare on Peter did not falter.

At one point, Margie had to go to the bathroom. Once she excused herself and shut the door, and Helena and Peter were alone, the atmosphere of the room became substantially more oppressive.

Helena didn't mince words. Keeping that glare on him, she quipped: "You like my daughter, Peter?"

Peter smiled nervously. "Yes. I like her very much."

She nodded. "Marjorie tells me that you intend to become a schoolteacher, is that right?"

"Yes, that's right. I'm working on my master's right now. I'd like to teach higher education."

Again, Helena smiled politely at him, but kept her gaze firm. "I've never known a teacher who was able to provide a comfortable living for a woman."

Unsure of how to respond to this, Peter just laughed nervously.

"I don't find what I said very funny." Helena's tone was like ice. "You'd better not waste my daughter's time, Mr. Murphy."

The bathroom door unlocked, and Margie stepped out. The couple stayed for about a half hour longer—the most awkward thirty minutes of Peter's life—before departing.

When they got in Peter's car, Margie asked: "So, what did my mother say to you while I was in the bathroom?"

"She told me that I would never be able to provide for you as a teacher."

Margie rolled her eyes. "That's so like her. I hate it when she does this. You kept your cool, didn't you?"

"I did."

"You're going to have a lot of shit-tests with her unfortunately, but if you keep passing, eventually she'll warm up to you. I don't like that she has to be like this, but at least you finally met her, for better or worse."

"I feel like she intends to sabotage our relationship."

"Don't worry." Margie leaned over and kissed him. "I won't let her keep you from me. We won't visit her often. I promise that she'll see the man I see in you eventually."

Needless to say, it would be years before that happened. On the few occasions Margie and Peter visited Helena, she always kept those resentful eyes on Peter and spoke to him in that cool tone. In a way it motivated him. He wanted to be successful, and to give Margie a house, a warm bed to sleep in, and plenty of food. He wanted to give a perfect life to his wife, not just to make her happy, but also so that he could say to her mother: *"You were wrong about me, Helena"*.

Peter stepped out of the bedroom, and then entered his daughter's room next. It was depressing to see her art no longer on display. All her paintings, easels, and works in progress were stacked inside the closet, almost shamefully.

It had been a lifelong dream for Peter to have a little girl. Why a daughter specifically? He didn't know. Maybe it was because he never had a sister growing up, or female cousins. Regardless, Margie had honored his dream.

Prior to her pregnancy, neither Margie nor Peter had considered children. Peter unloaded trucks at four in the morning and attended evening classes while Margie worked at a restaurant. When symptoms lead to a pregnancy test, there had been a mutual agreement without any argument to go ahead and have the child. It had been a confident decision on both their sides.

Peter had been there to witness the birth, along with Helena and Owen. It had a profound impact on him, watching the doctor deliver his first-born. It occurred to him that for the first time, he had witnessed someone's very beginning. The doctor handed the girl to Margie, who was drenched in sweat and was physically exhausted. It was then and there that she and Peter had decided on Erin Janelle for a name.

It was after Erin was born that Helena actually began warming up to Peter as well. Once the baby was taken to the maternity ward, Peter and Helena stepped out of the labor room and into the hall. Helena looked at him, but there wasn't that animosity he had always known in her eyes. There was something else. Peter didn't want to outright call it affection, but it was something close to that.

"That's a beautiful girl," she said. "A beautiful granddaughter."

"Yes, she most certainly is."

After a pause, Helena put her hand on his shoulder and said: "You've done well, Peter."

The Modern Prometheus

Just like that, the moment passed. His mother-in-law took her hand off him and went down the hall.

Owen had seen the exchange as he stepped out of the labor room. He laughed and said, "Damn, Peter. You finally got a compliment out of that old harpy."

All at once, everything in his life seemed beautiful. "Yeah," he said. "I guess I did."

Erin had always been an introspective and creative child. She wasn't interested in the toys or games that Peter brought home. She wasn't even excited about playing outside with soccer balls or exploring in the woods. For a while Peter was concerned about her lack of interest in anything. When you're a parent, any little thing could be a sign of something bad.

Peter eventually discovered his daughter's passion while she was sitting outside around the age of two. She was playing with a few daisies that she had plucked out of the fresh spring grass, chucking them in the air so that they blew around in the wind. Peter was watching her, lying in a lawn chair with his shirt off, sipping a beer and editing part of an essay on modernism and James Joyce. As he watched her, an idea struck him.

"Hey Erin!" he called, taking a blank piece of paper from his binder. "You want to see something cool?"

The little girl looked back at her father as he approached. He squatted down next to her and plucked a daisy up from nearby. "Watch this."

In one deft motion, he pressed the daisy against the paper and dragged it. A distinctive yellow smear appeared. Little Erin's eyes widened, amazed at what the flower had done. She tapped her fingers against the smear and made an excited cry. "How do that?" she babbled.

"That's called art," Peter told her, tossing the crushed flower away.

He took a few more daises and smeared them against his hand. He then pressed it against the paper, applied pressure, and pulled it away. A yellow handprint appeared.

Erin clapped and laughed.

"That's called paint, hun. You can make stuff appear with it. Your turn."

With two more daises, Peter gently smeared yellow against his daughter's hand, then had her press it against the blank side of the paper. Her little handprint appeared on it.

"Wow!" she exclaimed, laughing. "It magic!"

That was how Erin discovered that she wanted to become an artist.

Peter stepped out of his daughter's room and shut the door.

He suddenly remembered the fox under his arm. He held it before himself and looked into its worn, black eyes. Jack loved animals. Once, with a play doctor set complete with a plastic reflex hammer and stethoscope, he had lined up all his stuffed animals in his room and treated them for various pretend illnesses or ailments. Margie always (half-jokingly, he knew) said that maybe Jack would grow up to become a veterinarian, and that he'd—

Enough.

Peter pressed the fox to his chest. It was too much to think about Jack right now. There was still a lot he needed to do. He returned to his bedroom.

Most of his clothes were still in the closet—various dress shirts and slacks for work, along with T-shirts and jeans for when he wanted to dress casually. It seemed like maybe Margie was still attached to them, so she hadn't gotten rid of them yet. He undressed from the stolen clothes he'd gotten in Woodstock and put on a white T-shirt and jeans. Once he had a belt on, he slipped his pistol into the front of his pants and covered it with his shirt. He also took the obituary from the pocket of the stolen pants and slipped it into his own pocket.

There were two pairs of shoes on the floor of the closet, sneakers and professional leather ones. Peter slipped one sneaker onto his foot, and then took a moment to measure it against his new left foot. It felt strange, calling this other human being's body part his, but he supposed that he needed to begin doing it. His left foot was a full inch bigger than his right. He tried to slip the other sneaker on but was unsurprised and yet utterly annoyed that it didn't fit. He kicked the ill-fitting sneaker back into the closet, hearing the audible *thunk* as it hit the wall.

Guess I'm going about this half barefoot.

Margie's cell phone lay on the bedside table. Peter picked it up and eyed the home screen. It was 11 a.m. on June 20. He punched in the first number that came to mind and the phone unlocked. It bothered him that Margie still hadn't changed her phone code. She insisted that Peter know it in case of an emergency with the kids. Now though, it was convenient for the situation he was in.

The home screen was a photo of Peter holding Jack as a baby on his knee. Jack was nibbling on his fingers, looking at the camera with a little grin. When Peter checked the text inbox and recent phone calls, he thought it was peculiar that there seemed to be a three month gap in activity. Margie hadn't made any phone calls or texted anyone between early March and two days ago.

The recent texts were mostly back and forth stuff between Margie and her best friend Rachel, along with various work friends asking about how she was doing and if she needed anything. Rachel asked about Margie's stay at Hampstead.

Hampstead? Peter felt his intestines knot. *Isn't that that mental hospital up north? My wife was in a mental hospital for three months?*

After cycling through a few more texts, his suspicions were confirmed when he scrolled through the texts between Margie and Helena. Helena was telling Margie that Erin was going to be so happy when she finally sees her again, and that Erin was doing just fine.

Erin is in Manchester after all, with Helena. And I can bet any amount of money that Margie is up there too, now.

It looked like Owen had called a few hours ago as well. He also left a text: **MARGIE, HELENA SAID YOU WERE OUT FINALLY. GIVE ME A CALL.**

Owen, Peter thought. *Maybe you can help me. I could really use you right now.*

There was no telling where Peter's own phone was, but he supposed that his wife's would have to do. He slipped it into his pocket and took the charger from the outlet next to the bed. Along with this, he also dug out his wife's debit card from her purse, which sat on the floor in front of the bed. He figured that he would need money.

As Peter left the room, he carefully maneuvered around the broken mirror shards on the floor. Seeing them all, and the barely visible reflections within them, reminded him of the awful image he'd caught of himself in the mirror.

It had been an uncanny valley, looking at himself. There had been distinguishing features—the nose, mouth, eyebrows, and hair—that Peter recognized as himself. The rest was off structure, like staring at some deformed person you felt you could recognize but couldn't quite place who it was.

The worst of it all though, was The Expression.

There had been something in that face, buried deep within those eyes and the way his lips pulled back and how his eyebrows raised. A deep-rooted disturbance came out in The Expression, and out of everything in this nightmare, it was the thing that repulsed him the most.

The Expression hung in his mind as he stared at the shattered shards of mirror. Disgust and self-loathing filled his heart, and he went through the house smashing all the other mirrors, very careful to not gaze into any of them. When he approached the vanity mirror next to the bed, he looked away as he grabbed it and chucked it at a wall. Peter smashed the bathroom mirror by throwing an electric razor at it from a few feet away. He also destroyed the mirror in Erin's room from afar with a heavy ceramic mug. He didn't even spare the webcam on the family laptop. It was the best way for Peter to destroy The Expression besides destroying himself.

When he was sure that all the mirrors were destroyed, he took a moment to compose himself, and then thought over what he should do next. Just as he was about to leave, he suddenly felt a dull pain in the front of his head. He winced, pressing his hand against his forehead.

Good Christ, where did this headache come from?

Initially, he thought it was going to pass after a few moments, but it didn't. Instead, it got worse. That ache became throbbing, like the front of his brain was pulsating.

"What the hell is this?" he moaned.

With one hand still pressed against his forehead, he navigated back to the bathroom and dug through the medicine cabinet until he found a bottle of aspirin. He spilled a few pills into his mouth, chewed them up, and then sat on the toilet, waiting for the headache to pass. Slowly, it did.

Peter didn't have headaches often, and this one was worse than usual. He had been under a lot of stress lately, to say the least, but—

What if it has something to do with what's happened to my body?

He shook the aspirin. There were still plenty of pills in the bottle, so he pocketed it and finally stood. He supposed he would get answers soon.

Once ready, he stepped out of the house, got into the truck, and left the neighborhood.

22.

A college campus came into view on Elliot Street in Haverhill. A small concrete sign greeted all pulling into the visitor lot: NORTHERN ESSEX COMMUNITY COLLEGE.

Peter parked near several big steel MVRTA buses. The campus was familiar and yet felt alien at the same time. Besides his home on Argyle Street, this college campus was where Peter had spent most of his adult life.

A thought came to Peter. He checked the passenger dashboard compartment. Within were a few crumbled gum packets, a small pocketknife, two empty coffee cups, a handbook for the truck, a roll of duct tape, and a big pair of aviator sunglasses. He slipped the sunglasses on, and then ripped the rearview mirror off and pitched it out the window.

It probably wouldn't do much, but the sunglasses brought a sense of security to Peter. With them on, The Expression would at least be partially hidden from the world around him. It also helped that it was late afternoon, and most of the morning and afternoon classes were dismissed. It was also a summer semester, so there wouldn't be as many students around. There would be some people about, but not a lot.

Northern Essex Community College was nothing extra like some Ivy League universities. Concrete paths and stairs connected a series of modestly sized brick buildings with wide windows that peered into classrooms that weren't much indistinguishable from ordinary high school classrooms.

Peter liked this school and campus. He'd spent one autumn at the Durham campus of the University of New Hampshire, and he didn't take to the culture of the place—too highbrow, pretentious and self-righteous. He enjoyed teaching at community college. Everything was more laid back, and the students were usually older, diverse, and willing to learn. He could be himself here and befriend students and faculty who were academic but also humble.

Peter circled around the Behrakis Student Center, where the cafeteria and front desk were. He crossed a large open lawn that rolled up and down hilly knolls towards the Spurk Building, where the humanities were taught. That's where his office was—at least, that's where it *had* been when he was still alive.

Peter's passion for education came from virtually nowhere. Academia was nowhere to be found on either his mother or father's side. Dad came from a long line of fishermen and Mom's family just took whatever job they could. Dad had left behind all his old books before he left, most from Ireland: O'Brien, Shaw, and McGahern, along with the poetry of Seamus Heaney. Growing up, Peter had gobbled up these books, and they gave him a sense of guidance that he otherwise wouldn't have gotten in the absence of a father. He had decided to become a teacher because he believed that the humanities could help and heal people in ways that medication could not.

He entered the Spurk Building, and walked down its wide corridors, with their painted brick walls, plaster floors, and concrete ceilings with fluorescent lights. Upon entering the lobby, he discovered a little mural set up in the center of the room. A photograph of him—specifically a print of his autumn ID—was set up on a big bulletin board. Under the photo was a eulogy of sorts.

"In Memoriam – Professor Peter K. Murphy 1983 – 2020. Spurk remembers fondly Professor Murphy who passed away just before Christmas last year. Peter taught Romantic and Irish literature, as well as English Comp and Intro to American Philosophy. Every summer he organized poetry workshops to give Haverhill poets a voice and helped with the campus literary magazine. He is fondly remembered. Donations can be made upstairs near the conference room to support his family in their time of need."

Dozens of signatures and messages were written in sharpie or pen around the memorial. Peter read a few: "REST IN POWER PROF M!"; "MURPH, THANK YOU FOR INTRODUCING ME TO MY KINDRED SPIRIT EDNA O'

BRIEN!"; "SPURK FEELS EMPTIER WITHOUT YOU, PETER! RIP!"

That last message was signed by Marissa Lopez. Peter pressed a hand against his chest, suddenly touched. Marissa had been an orphan from Ecuador raised by a foster family. She was paying for her education almost entirely out of pocket. Peter had been working with her after every class to help with her essays just prior to his death. Was she okay? Were things better for her? There were names and signatures he recognized from other students and colleagues as well.

All this was too much. Peter stepped away from the board.

There was a staircase in the lobby that led to the second and third floors. Peter took them up to the third. His office was directly next to Theresa Gimmel's office, his closest compatriot in the literature department.

Theresa had been working at the school just as long as Peter had, and together they had kept the literary department on its feet, and also organized the poetry slams and campus literary magazine. Theresa taught Russian literature, mostly Dostoevsky, Tolstoy, Akhmatova and several other names that Peter had no hope pronouncing or remembering.

Theresa's office was locked, and the light inside was off. He approached his own office door and found it unlocked. He took a few moments to mentally prepare himself, and then he opened the door, reached in, and turned the light on.

Almost nothing remained in his office except for his desk and old uncomfortable chair, still splitting at the seams with yellow foam dribbling out. His big map of Ireland and poster of Gaelic phrases were taken off the walls, and his knick-knacks and framed photos of Erin's paintings were gone as well.

A stack of cardboard boxes sat in the corner of the room. Peter opened the flap of the box on top and saw all his office supplies in it. A note was stapled to the flap:

Dr. Gimmel, I ask if you're able to do something with Professor Murphy's belongings. I've contacted his wife, but she refuses to take anything. I don't know what use his things have for the school. Would you mind taking them? I understand you and Peter were close. I must begin making room for the new philosophy professor. Peter's old office would be an ideal location for her.

It was signed by the administrator, Lionel Sandler. Peter crumbled the note up bitterly.

"Excuse me."

Peter nearly leapt out of his skin. Theresa Gimmel stood in the doorway, and she scowled at him with a mixed expression of pain and offense.

Peter opened his mouth but was unable to get any words out. Theresa's presence had caught him off guard.

"What are you doing here?" she asked.

"I was looking for Professor Murphy."

"Who are you? Why are you wearing sunglasses indoors?"

"Listen, Dr. Gimmel—"

"How do you know who I am?"

"I'm sorry, I was just looking for the man who teaches Irish lit here. My daughter took one of his classes, and…"

Theresa stepped forward and pulled Peter away from the boxes by his sleeve. "Sir, Professor Murphy is not here right now. You are trespassing in his office and are digging through his property. I advise that you leave right now."

What was he supposed to say? He looked into her eyes and saw the pain of his death in them. She had become protective of whatever material possessions he had left behind as well as his reputation.

"I just wanted to give my condolences," he managed. "I didn't know Professor Murphy personally, but what happened to him… it just—it wasn't right. That's all. I'm sorry for your loss."

Theresa swallowed. "He was my friend."

"I'm sorry. I'll go."

Peter stepped out but didn't make it far down the corridor before Theresa stopped him: "Sir, wait a minute!"

Theresa approached him, grimacing as she stared at his face. There was a flicker of shock in her eyes as she examined him—

she was seeing something in him that she recognized, but her expression was pure disbelief. Maybe she did recognize him a little, but Peter had a feeling that the deformities and structure of his face were throwing her off, along with the sunglasses.

"Who did you say you were?" she said.

"My daughter took one of Professor Murphy's classes and I had a question regarding her grade."

"You didn't call advising?"

"I live just down the street."

Theresa squinted, and then her eyes looked down at his new bare foot. Awkwardly, Peter hid it behind his other foot and his hands clenched into fists.

"Sir, I'd like you to leave this campus immediately, or I'll call security."

"No problem. I'm sorry."

Peter turned on his heel and rushed down the hall. He felt his old friend's stare on him until he went down the stairs and was out of sight.

As he scurried across the campus back to the parking lot, Peter couldn't help but feel emotional. He thought about all the times he and Theresa would stay in the cafeteria for hours at a time after class, just talking. They talked about everything together; about love, politics, their dreams, and their families. One time, Tessa told him—

The Modern Prometheus

Peter suddenly stopped in his tracks. Tessa? That wasn't her name. *Wait, what? Who was I just thinking about?*

What just happened?

Peter blinked and looked all around himself. He was surrounded by brick buildings with wide windows, and he stood on a wide concrete path in a large open field. It looked like a school, but he didn't know where it was or what he was doing here. He started to panic.

What just happened? What was I just thinking about? WHERE AM I? HOW DID I GET HERE?

His head started to hurt. He shook a few aspirin into his palm and swallowed them. As he screwed the cap back on, he closed his eyes and tried to recollect himself.

Theresa. Theresa Gimmel, not Tessa. He opened his eyes, and realized that he was at Northern Essex Community College. He remembered why he had come here, and his recent encounter with his old friend. *Theresa, that's her name. Not Tessa.*

Grimly, Peter returned the aspirin to his pocket and stood rubbing his temples, bewildered at himself.

Holy hell, what happened to me? I suddenly just became disoriented and confused, and then I completely forgot who I was thinking about and where I was.

Did I just suffer some sort of memory lapse or something?

Peter swallowed. The ache in his head numbed as the aspirin took hold, and he started to feel a little more clear-headed. He took a moment to remember where he had been going, and then recalled that he was heading towards the parking lot to leave.

I've got to get my head on straight. I feel like I'm losing my grip.

He made his way back to the truck and left the campus.

23.

Peter spent several hours sitting in the truck in an empty rest stop next to the interstate. Sometimes he got angry, ranting and raving to himself within the privacy of the vehicle. Other times he fell into hysterical crying fits, clutching Mr. Fox to his chest and begging for an answer to why all this was happening. Most of the time, he was silent, too confused and disassociated to be angry or hurt.

It felt as if the laws of nature had been destroyed, and everything he had been taught about existence through science and philosophy was a lie. It was a tormenting limbo to be in, feeling as if you had once understood everything for your entire life, only to have your world suddenly become incongruous and oppressive. A world filled with unknowns and impossibilities.

Mostly, he kept thinking about that weird memory lapse he had experienced as he was leaving the college campus. While the headache had mostly subsided, he still felt faint stings now and then inside his forehead. It did no favors for his anxiety, and it motivated him to continue pursuing what few diminishing options he had left.

At around eight, when daylight finally faded, Peter fueled the truck at the nearest station, paying for it at the pump with his wife's debit card, then drove to Lowell. On Union Street he parked on the side of the road across from a small duplex. A single porch light glowed above one of the front doors—his brother's front door.

It seemed foolish to try and do this. Maybe it was because he was in a confused and vulnerable state of mind, but he felt that he needed to be close to blood family. He needed to know if there was still a connection between Peter Murphy and the world.

Peter stepped out of the truck, crossed the street, and stepped onto the porch. Moths danced around the light over the door, and their abstract shadows played against the surroundings. He saw a fold out chair set up next to the door, and empty beer bottles and cans surrounded it.

This was not comforting to see. Owen had sworn off drinking back in 2015 when it cost him his wife. That had been an ugly divorce, and Owen had never touched a drop since.

Peter dreaded going inside and seeing what all this had done to his brother.

Peter tried the door and found it unlocked. He stepped inside and followed the stench of liquor to the kitchen. Empty bottles and cans littered the table and counters. Sitting alone at the table in the dim light of an overhead lamp was Owen. His hair was a dirty thinning mop atop his scalp, and his face looked barely distinguishable. He wore nothing but a pair of boxers and it looked like he had gained weight.

"Owen," Peter whispered from the doorway.

His brother didn't move.

Peter banged his fist against the frame. "Owen!"

Owen snorted, looked around the room, then his eyes settled on Peter's silhouette in the darkness. His eyes were glassed over with drunkenness and grief.

"Who the fuck are you?" Owen said.

Peter struggled to answer. "Owen, what happened to you?"

Owen scoffed, shook his head, and stood up. "The fuck is this? I told you fuckers already! I'll be quiet! I know you just had a baby. I'll keep the god damn noise down! You didn't have to barge into my fucking house!"

"Owen, I'm not a neighbor."

"Then get outta here! Who are you? Why the fuck are you wearing sunglasses? You some hippie trying to rob me again?

What else you want?" He laughed and rolled his eyes. "Of course I forgot to lock the fucking door. Whatever. Take what you want. I don't care."

Owen dug into the fridge, took out a six pack of beer and set it on the table. He tore a can off the rings and opened it.

"Owen, why are you doing this to yourself?"

"I can do whatever I damn well please, motherfucker."

"You quit drinking after Jasmine left."

Owen lifted the can to his mouth but stopped just short of pressing it to his lips. Slowly, he brought the can down. "Excuse me?"

"Your ex-wife, Jasmine. You met her at a Bruins game in 2008. You got married a year later and lived in Lowell together."

"How the fuck—"

"She left you, Owen." Peter stepped forward into the weak kitchen light. "She left you because you were depressed after Mom died, and you drank because of it. It pushed her away. After she left, you swore off drinking, hoping that she'd come back. She never did, but you stayed sober. You stayed on the wagon for your niece and nephew's sake. Jack and Erin were the closest things to children of your own."

"Listen, prick. I don't—"

Peter dropped the bombshell: "You stopped drinking for my sake. For the sake of my wife, Margie."

Those glassy drunk eyes widened. Owen's face became as still and white as a marble bust. Then he chuckled and dropped the beer to the floor. It foamed out all over the tiles.

"Oh man." Owen covered his face with his hands. "This is—this is some serious fucking Ebenezer Scrooge shit, man."

Peter did something then that he swore he wouldn't do. He took the sunglasses off and stared at his brother. The Expression was no longer hidden.

"Look at me," Peter said. "It's me. It's your brother, Peter. I'm alive. I'm here."

Owen didn't look.

"God damn it, Owen. Look at me. I am your older brother. We shared the same bed together until we were nearly ten years old. Dad left us, and Mom thought he joined the IRA. You work in construction and busted my balls for years when I said I wanted to become a teacher. You called me a dweeb, but I knew you were proud of me."

"No."

"When I was eight and you were six, we threw around a baseball in the apartment and broke a decorative rocking horse that Mom loved. She spanked us both to hell and back for that."

"I can't hear this shit. No, sir."

"You were there for the birth of my daughter, Erin. You were holding Margie's hand when it happened. You saw Helena approve of me outside the labor room afterwards, and you cracked a joke about it."

"Shut your goddamned mouth!"

"Mom cried out for Grandma!" Peter pressed. "When we took her to High Pointe Hospice House, she cried out for Grandma just before she died. We were both there. We were holding her hands."

"Fucking stop!"

Owen snatched an empty beer bottle out of the sink and chucked it at Peter. The bottle hit the wall next to him, shattering on impact. Owen scowled at Peter, looking directly into The Expression.

"I saw my brother's dead body," he said, his voice shrill. "After the accident, they had me come in to identify the body because Margie couldn't do it. I saw those whites that were his eyes. No life. I watched my brother's urn get buried in a hole along with my goddamned nephew's casket. I watched them both get buried! I don't know who you are, but you are not my brother. Now get the fuck out of my house! Get out!"

"Owen, I—"

"Out!" He pitched another bottle. "Get out of my life, you fucking imposter! You fucking ghost! Get out! Go!"

Peter slipped his sunglasses back on and slowly crept out of the kitchen. He stepped out of the duplex, and he could hear his brother sobbing within as he shut the door.

There was nothing left. The world considered him dead. Peter crossed the street and got into the truck. If he had any more tears left, he would have shed them, but by that point he was dried out. Now he was just empty.

Using Margie's phone, he opened the GPS and set a destination for Woodstock, back to that awful place. He placed the phone on the dashboard and gripped the steering wheel. This whole endeavor was a mistake. He'd done nothing but bring more suffering upon his loved ones.

Just as he was about to put the truck into drive, he stopped himself. Something felt funny on his arm. He turned on the overhead light and looked at it. A strange red rash had formed on his skin just below his wrist. Peter scratched it, and a small drop of blood emerged.

"What the hell?"

He wiped the blood off on his pant leg. He needed to see Jacob again, as much as he detested the idea. Something was happening to his body and his mind.

The Modern Prometheus

III.
FAMILY

24.

A few blocks from South Willow Street—an absurdly clustered and noisy drag of road that was the first commercial district for anyone entering Manchester from the south—stood a quaint neighborhood with narrow streets and small houses. About a mile up Piscataquog Street in this neighborhood, at mailbox number fourteen, sat a single-story white home with a little yard decorated with tacky lawn gnomes and plastic flamingos. This was the residence of Helena Strauss.

It was furnished with antiquated tables and couches from the late eighties. Helena was a meticulous woman, determined to never waste money on anything if she could use what she already had until it fell to splinters. The polish on the wooden chairs and tables were chipped and scraped, the cushions on the couch were sunken in, and the only source of electronic entertainment was an old television with a VCR.

Roughly around the time Peter crawled into the bathtub at his home in Atkinson upon discovering what he had become, Helena Strauss was sitting on the couch in her living room, knitting. This was a hobby that she had taken up recently to pass the time. She knitted little animals mostly, and had even set up a wicker basket on the coffee table filled with little octopuses, lions, cats, bears and pigs. It was a pleasant way to keep her mind from wandering. In recent months, her mind wandered an awful lot. Sitting around watching TV was doing little favors for her when she wasn't preoccupied with taking care of Erin.

Just as she was finishing the last few loops of a knitted dog, a car was heard speeding up her street and furiously pulling into her driveway. A car door opened and slammed shut, and moments later a hard knock came against her front door. Helena set her needles aside and went to the door—keeping the chain on but turning the knob lock—and opened it.

The haggard and terrified face of her daughter Margie gaped at her. Her hair was in her face, and her bulging eyes peered out from between messy strands.

"Mom, let me in."

"What?" She quickly undid the chain and opened the door completely. "Sweetheart, are you all right?"

Margie rushed in and looked around, as if convinced something was hiding somewhere. "Did you see anything?" she asked.

"What are you talking about, Margie?"

"There was—I don't—I don't know how—"

"Honey, calm down." Helena put her hands on her daughter's shoulders.

"I don't know what just happened."

"What? What happened?"

Margie choked up. "I saw him."

"You saw who?"

"Peter."

The moment the name passed her lips, embarrassment washed over Margie's face, and she covered her eyes with her hands. She started crying.

"Marjorie, sweetheart. Come here."

Helena took Margie into her arms and her daughter cried into the bend of her neck.

"I feel like I've finally lost it. I'm crazy," she sobbed.

"You are not crazy."

"I saw him, Mom." Margie pulled herself off and looked earnestly into her mother's eyes. "He was right there. I saw Peter. I heard something moving around the house. I went to our bedroom, and he was right there. He *touched* me. I felt it."

"You saw Peter," Helena said slowly. "In your house? And he touched you?"

"Yes!" Margie nearly shouted. She looked away and shook her head. "It couldn't have been real, but God, it felt so real."

"Honey, sit down. I'll make you some tea."

Margie sat on the couch. Mentally, she floated like a buoy stranded in a vast sea and stared at the basket of little animals on the coffee table. Her mother had told her of the hobby over the phone a while back, but she was only now just seeing it for the first time. It made her think about just how long she had been away from this house, and how long she had been away from her daughter as well.

Helena finished making a cup of oolong tea, and she returned to her daughter and handed it to her.

"Thank you," Margie said, noticing how hot the cup was in her cold hands.

"Now, let's take a few steps back." Helena sat down next to her. "What exactly happened?"

Margie held the teacup up to her lips, but realized that she had no desire to drink anything, so she kept it in her lap to keep herself warm. "I was just… I was in the bathroom. And I thought I heard footsteps, and someone yelling in the house. I went to the bedroom, and…" An exasperated sigh left her. "I thought I saw him. Peter. Except he looked—something was off about him. He looked deformed. Like something was wrong with him." Margie cut herself short. She placed the tea on the coffee table and got choked up again.

Helena rubbed her back. "It's okay, honey."

"I feel like I saw a ghost."

"Maybe it's a side effect of the medication?"

"I don't care what it was! I want him back, Mom. I want my son back. I want my husband back. I want them both back."

From the guest bedroom, Erin watched the scene unfold from a crack in the door. She felt chilled by what she was seeing and hearing. This was the first time she had seen her mother in a long time, and what she was saying disturbed her. She shut the door and pressed her back against it.

What was she saying about Dad? She saw him? How could she have seen Dad? Erin couldn't help but feel angry at Mom for insinuating that Dad was still somehow alive, as if she wanted to tease her. Erin knew her father was gone. She knew her brother was gone, too.

For the past three months, this small house had become Erin's home. Grandma Helena had set up the guest bedroom for her to live in. It had once been Mom's room as a little girl, and Erin slept on her mother's old bed with its blue sheets and rickety old frame, surrounded by her mother's girlhood dolls and stuffed animals. It was a surreal experience. Erin had visited

Grandma for the holidays and had been aware of this room, but actually living in it was a level of intimacy that she didn't feel ready for.

The past six months had altered the course of Erin's entire life. There had been no way to predict or prepare for it in any way. As far as her young mind could comprehend, there was the Erin of *before*, and then the Erin of *now*. One life vanished, and the other emerged after Dad and Jack died.

Life had been perfect, before everything happened; there was no other way to describe it. She had had two parents that loved her dearly and gave her everything she ever wanted or needed. She had been closer to her father than to her mother, and this made her feel guilty sometimes. Mom was someone who helped her with her homework, made her breakfast before school, and nurtured her when she was sick, but she wasn't supportive of her artistic ambitions. In fact, they seemed to confuse her.

"Your mother has always been like that," Dad had told her once. "She's always been more left brained than right."

"What's that mean?" Erin had asked.

"It means she likes things that are logical and make sense. If you're right brained, then you like things that are abstract and not always logical, like art. It's why your mother works with computers and I'm a teacher."

"Why did you two get married, then?"

Dad had laughed at that. "Beats me, kid. Love works like that sometimes."

Dad had fully embraced Erin's artistic endeavors, taking her out to craft stores, critiquing her work, and taking her to museums. In a lot of ways, she painted mostly for him. Her father had become her audience. For hours, she would lock herself away in her room and paint anything that came to her mind. She painted the trees in the backyard, the neighbor's cat, or scenes from the fantasy books that she had read. Once she finished a piece and the paint dried, she would drape her latest work in a blanket, and would eagerly pull Dad into her room and have him sit down in a chair before the clothed easel.

"And now, the latest work from Erin Murphy!" she would monologue like a showman, before tearing the blanket off to unveil her creation.

Dad would always laugh, cover his mouth, and sometimes even stand up and applaud her. He would kneel beside her and give his personal critique of the work. "The blues you use evoke melancholic bliss" was one thing he said. "The sky and the birds on the power-line contrast with one another beautifully" was another critique that she remembered.

Always, he was proud of her. He took the paintings she made and hung them in the living room and hallways, so anyone who visited could see them. It was incredibly validating. Once, he even told her that they could take her work to an art show when she was older.

That'll never happen now, Erin thought gloomily.

As well as a wonderful father, Erin had had the best little brother any young girl could ever ask for. When Mom and Dad initially told her that she was going to have a little brother, she absolutely hated the idea. She had resented the concept of not being her parents' only child and had even threatened to run away from home a few times.

Yet, when her parents finally came home from the hospital with baby Jack in his carrier, her attitude had changed. Her parents had called her into the living room, and Erin reluctantly left her room, not wanting anything to do with the new addition to the Murphy family.

"Erin, come say hello to your little brother," Mom said.

Dad carefully set the carrier down on the floor and unbuckled the baby. Erin eyed the child, marveled, and she felt no resentment. Baby Jack slept, and one of his little fingers was in his mouth, sucking it. He seemed totally unaware of his surroundings, enraptured in some infant musing, undisturbed by the world.

"Be careful," Mom said. "He was very fussy as we were leaving the hospital."

Dad took the baby out of the carrier and beckoned Erin to come closer. Erin did so, and her father gently placed the baby in her arms. He was much heavier than she had been expecting, and it took a little of her strength to keep him still. She looked into his snoozing face, and he made a little hiccup sound. Erin was mesmerized.

So, I'm a big sister, she thought at the time. Whatever displeasure she felt faded as she admired her little brother. Maybe not having Mom and Dad's complete and undivided attention all the time wouldn't be so bad. It just meant that she had the attention of a baby now, too.

Jack seemed to adore Erin. He got very upset whenever she wasn't around. When the family was in the living room and Jack was free to crawl around, he always gravitated towards her. Erin never missed an opportunity to feed him or bathe him. By the time Jack was old enough to walk, she would play with him in the backyard, pulling him around in the little red wagon or building castles with him out of twigs and leaves, flexing her artistic creativity to try and inspire him. She wanted to be as much of an influence on him as Mom and Dad were. When he grew old enough, perhaps she could even teach him how to paint, too.

It was a gift to be an older sister. For two and a half years, having a brother had been her favorite thing in the whole world.

Now that Jack was gone, she didn't know what she was anymore, and this was made all the worse now that her father was gone too.

Dead.

Even now, the word chilled her. The concept of death had always been something that she was aware of—she saw it in movies and read about it in books—but it had always seemed like some fabled concept, a myth, something often talked about but rarely ever experienced. Now that death had been experienced, Erin felt as if she understood it very well, and nothing terrified her more than death. One moment you exist; the next, you become nothing more than a memory.

Erin remembered the night Dad and Jack died. It was something she went over in her head again and again, sometimes to the point where she couldn't sleep.

It had been a few days before Christmas, and she and Mom were in the living room decorating the tree. Mom was going around it, wrapping it in tinsel, and Erin was putting on little elf and sled ornaments.

Dad stuck his head into the room. "I'm taking Jack out. He's gonna help me pick out a gift for Helena."

Jack trotted into the room and stood by Dad's leg, playing with his little fox stuffed animal that he called Mr. Fox.

"I'm sure anything is better than that *Entertainment Weekly* subscription you got her last year," Mom said. "I still hear her bemoaning it to this day."

"That's what I'm hoping to avoid. We'll be back in probably an hour."

"Bye, Dad! Bye, Jack!" Erin said. "We'll have the tree done by the time you get back."

"Sounds good. I'm sure you'll make it look beautiful." Dad hunched down and took Jack up in one of his arms. "Wish us luck."

"Getting a gift for my mom?" Mom quipped. "You'll need more than luck."

That made Dad laugh, and then he stepped out of the room. That was the last time Erin had ever seen him or her brother.

They didn't come back in an hour. After an hour and a half, Mom tried calling and left a few texts. A full two hours later, the police knocked on the front door.

Erin watched the whole thing unfold from the kitchen. Mom sat on the couch in the living room as the two police officers talked to her. Erin couldn't comprehend what was happening. When the two cops left, Mom wandered into the kitchen like a phantom and looked blankly at Erin. Never had she ever seen such an expression in her mother's face before.

"Your father and brother are dead," she said weakly, her eyes far away and her face full of shock. She left the kitchen, went to her bedroom down the hall and shut the door.

Dead? The reality of it didn't hit Erin. It didn't hit her in the days leading up to the funeral services, either. It was like she had fallen off a steep cliff and was descending to an uncertain fate. Hanging in limbo, unable to fully process what had actually happened to her family.

It had been at the wake when Erin stopped falling and it all hit her at once. Dad had been cremated. Mom explained that cremation was when a dead person's body was burned into ashes. The ashes were then placed in something called an urn, and Dad's urn was a marble gray box with a picture of him on it that read: "PETER K. MURPHY – 1983 – 2020". When Erin asked why Dad was cremated, Mom said it was because that's what he had wanted.

Jack wasn't cremated. He was put in a casket, but it was left closed during the service. Mom said that she didn't want Jack to be cremated, but she couldn't bear to look at him, either. Throughout the service, Mom fell into hysterics. She would be all right for a few hours, but every once in a while, she would leap from her seat and start putting her hands on the urn and the casket, sobbing her eyes out, shouting Dad and Jack's names.

"Give them back to me!" she would scream. "I want my husband! I want my child! Don't take them away from me!"

That had been when it hit Erin. *I'm never going to see Dad or baby brother again.* It came to her so completely and clearly, seeing her mother like this. In an instant she was overwhelmed. When Grandma Helena managed to placate Mom and talk her back to her seat, Erin got up and ran to the bathroom. She locked herself in a stall and began screaming. She banged her fists against the walls of that stall, slammed the toilet seat against the rim of the bowl, and slapped herself in the face.

I'm never going to see Dad or my baby brother again. It kept repeating in her head, and every time it did, the more anguished and angrier she became. It was like she was imploding.

Erin wasn't sure how long she had been in that bathroom stall, but she knew that she only stopped self-destructing when Grandma Helena yanked open the door with a look of horror on her face.

"Good Christ, child! What are you doing to yourself?"

"I don't want to say goodbye to my dad and brother!" Erin bawled.

Grandma Helena's chin quivered, and she pulled Erin out of the stall and began running a sink faucet. She dabbed some water on Erin's face and wiped blood off her nose with a paper towel. When she had been cleaned up, Grandma Helena squeezed Erin in her arms.

"I'm so sorry, child," she whispered to her. "I'm so sorry that you have to experience this."

After the funeral, Mom tried her best to function as a mother. She still went to work, made breakfast, helped with schoolwork and cleaned. Grandma Helena visited twice a week and always offered to help, but Mom always dismissed her.

"You shouldn't try to take all this on alone, Margie," Grandma Helena had told her. "I'm here for you if you need anything at all."

"I know, Mom," Mom had replied. "But so long as I keep busy, stay focused, I'll be fine."

Hesitantly, Grandma hadn't pressed the matter further.

After about a month, though, Mom began to fall apart. One moment she was talking casually with Erin, and then the next she was crying. She started spending entire days lying in her bed, clutching the pillows on Dad's side, surrounded by crumpled tissues. Other times she locked herself in Jack's room, and Erin could hear her talking to herself in there, as if she were trying to communicate with her dead son. She had stopped going out for groceries as well, and the house became nearly depleted of food by the time winter ended. Erin began a diet of dry cereal straight from the box, and when that ran out, she moved on to dry rice.

The breaking point came in early March. One afternoon, while Mom was sleeping on the couch, the doorbell rang. Mom grunted and turned over, clearly uninterested in getting up, so Erin answered the door. It was Grandma Helena.

The moment she saw her, Grandma's eyes widened. "Good Lord," she said, kneeling in front of Erin. "Look how thin you are! And your hair and clothes are filthy. Child, when was the last time you ate something?"

Erin shrugged. "I don't know."

Offense crossed her grandmother's face. "I'm going to speak with your mother, Erin."

Grandma entered the house and found Mom on the couch. She stormed over and shook her awake.

"What? Who? Erin, leave me alone," Mom said hoarsely.

"It's your mother, Marjorie."

Mom sat up, rubbing her head and groaning. "Oh Christ."

"We need to have a word." Grandma turned to Erin. "Erin, go to your room, please. We need to speak mother to mother."

Erin left them. She stayed in her room for a good hour, lying in bed and staring at the ceiling. Every now and then she got up and opened her door a crack to peek down the hall into the living room. She could see Grandma sitting on a chair across from where Mom sat on the couch. Mom shook her head a lot, and they spoke softly to each other.

Eventually, footsteps approached Erin's door and a knock rapped against it. Erin got off her bed and opened it. Mom stood before her, and Grandma was behind her with her arms crossed.

"Hi honey," Mom said.

"Hi," Erin said.

Mom struggled to say something. She wiped her mouth and ran her fingers through Erin's hair. "Listen, babe. Grandma and I have been talking. I know things haven't been well since what happened. We both haven't been good. Grandma thinks I need help, to get myself together. She thinks that it's best if you stay with her for a little while."

"But why?" It was upsetting for Erin to hear this. She didn't want to be away from Mom, even if she had been behaving the way she had.

Mom bit her lip. It was clear that this was not easy for her, either. "I need to go to a hospital."

"What? Why?"

"It's not like a hospital you go to when you've got a broken bone or anything like that. It's the sort of hospital that helps you heal the way you feel. There are a lot of things I need healed. And when I'm there, doctors can give me medication and therapy to help me."

"Your mother is going to work on being a mother again," Grandma said sympathetically. "It's very difficult for her after what happened to your brother and father."

It's difficult to be anything after what happened to Dad and Jack, Erin thought bitterly.

Mom put a hand on Erin's shoulder. "It'll just be for a little while, Erin. While I'm in there, I'm going to try and call you as much as I can. When I'm out, we'll live together here again, and we're going to try to get through this. Okay?"

Erin hated the idea. Yet, as she looked into Mom's face, which was so vulnerable and broken, she couldn't say no. A whimper left Erin, and she hugged her.

"I just want everything to be okay again," she said.

"I do too, honey," Mom told her. "It's all I want. Just a little time, for me to get back on my feet. Grandma Helena will cook for you, help you study, and make sure you're taken care of while I recover. Know that I love you and I'm not abandoning you, sweetheart. Okay?"

"Okay," Erin said.

"A little while" turned into three months. Mom did call at least once a week for fifteen minutes—it was as much as the hospital allowed—but Erin couldn't find anything to talk about, and the conversations always became awkward silences broken up by small talk. If anything, the phone calls only made her feel worse afterwards.

Finally, Erin pulled herself off the door and went to a little desk by the window. The desk was covered in over a dozen books that Erin had plucked off her grandmother's bookshelf, started, and never finished. It was difficult for her to read. Her mind wandered when she tried to focus, and even when she was able to read, she found that she was unable to remember anything. She just couldn't do it, not in her mindset. There was not much else to do in this house besides watch TV, but Erin couldn't even do that. All trails seemed to end with that December night Jack and Dad had ceased to exist.

Erin sat at the desk and rested her cheeks in her palms, staring out the window at the street. There were dark clouds out, and it looked like it had begun to rain. The texture of the sidewalks and street darkened as they got wet. Someone walking on the sidewalk picked up the pace, holding a newspaper over their head as the rain grew more intense.

Nothing mattered anymore. Erin had lost her passion for art, for love, for the future—everything. She hadn't picked up a paintbrush since December and had put her easel and all her paintings in her closet back in January. It hurt to even look at them, knowing that Dad wasn't around and would never take her to an art show.

It also became difficult to relate to the other kids at school. Everything they talked about—boys, makeup, sleepovers—all seemed superfluous and annoying now. She distanced herself from everyone, even when her friends complained. She just didn't want to be around them.

The only thing Erin wanted more than anything else in the world was to have her family back. Only now she realized that she had taken so much for granted. How tightly her father used to hug her, or how prickly his face felt as he kissed her when he hadn't shaved. She missed picking Jack up and swinging him around while he laughed and screamed, making her feel like the strongest big sister in the world. She missed when they used to chase each other around in the backyard pretending to be dinosaurs or teaching him how to build castles.

As far as she was concerned, she had every right in the world to hate God.

25.

On the morning of June 21, old folks wandered the sidewalks of main drag in Woodstock to open their shops, set their flags out, or chat while having a smoke. The town was not slow to wake. It operated on a firm schedule, where everyone woke up around the same time to get their businesses going or go about their usual routines.

Among those who emerged that morning was a young, boyish doctor with light blonde hair and glasses with comically thick lenses. Nobody in town presumed that he was a doctor just by outward appearance—he seemed too youthful and wore plain clothes, usually flannel and slacks. Nobody even knew his full name—they just knew him as *Jacob*.

Jacob had appeared in town seemingly out of the blue. One day starting in early January, the young man began going to Daisy's Diner at seven o'clock every morning. The bell over the door would ring and Daisy Miller would seat him.

"Same as usual, Jacob?" Daisy would ask.

Jacob would just nod. "Same per usual."

Daisy would poke her head into the kitchen to tell Jacques the order, which was always Eggs Benedict, black coffee and a side of toast. Nothing more, nothing less.

Jacob's temperament was always reserved. Daisy would read her book behind the counter while she waited on the young man's food. Jacob would scribble in a notebook, never taking his eyes off the paper except to thank Daisy when the food arrived, to eat, and to pay her. One time, she had caught a glance at what he was working on, which were complicated math equations and diagrams, but the sight was short lived, as Jacob closed his notebook and set it on the seat beside him.

"What are you working on?" she had prodded gently.

"Just something for school."

"Oh? You're in school?"

"Sort of. I'm conducting research in the area."

"Like what?"

"Just nature."

"Like birds?"

"Just nature," he said with a dismissive smile. "Thank you."

That's how it had been for the past five and a half months. Through the grapevine, it seemed that he only ever went to Daisy's Diner and sometimes Earl's convenience store next door, but that was it. Grace Wylde, who ran the only motel in town, said that the young man wasn't one of her guests. Nobody knew where he was staying, but it must have been close by.

Many in town were curious about this stranger, but they were more entertained by the gossip they conjured up about him. Some said that he was a federal agent investigating the drug trade at the Canadian border; others said that he was a criminal in hiding; few others believed that maybe he was some sort of journalist.

The truth, which nobody knew, was that Dr. Jacob Abbott was not a journalist, nor a criminal, or a special agent. He wasn't even a student. It was true that he had received a research grant from the university he had graduated from, but he was a medical doctor—at least, theoretically. And while he *was* conducting research in the area, it had nothing to do with Woodstock and its mundane way of life. It was about the secrets of life and death.

At eight o' clock on the morning of June 21, the man known as Jacob stepped out of Daisy's Diner and stood on the sidewalk, eyeing the main drag of Woodstock up and down. There was a big ugly bruise on his nose that was still purple. Daisy had remarked on it while taking his order, but Jacob had shrugged it off and said that he had accidentally fallen down the stairs the day before. Daisy hadn't pressed it.

With every dull throb Jacob felt in his nose, he thought of Peter.

That morning he was particularly exhausted. These past few months had been incredibly nerve-wracking. For weeks he'd been cooped up inside his workspace with almost no human interaction, going out only for necessities, always paranoid that somebody was watching him. When he was far enough along with the project, his own health had stopped mattering to him. The only thing that did matter was success.

Earl, the owner of the convenience store next door, stepped outside and lit a cigarette. The old man eyed Jacob, and then went about his smoking in silence. Jacob had become accustomed to the stares he got the few times he was ever in Woodstock during the day.

Jacob crossed the street, took a twenty-minute walk through town, then went up the forest trail he'd become so familiar with over the past several months. After about twenty-five yards, the cabin appeared.

Ever since Peter got away, Jacob began to resent everything about this small wooden cabin. What was once excitement was now oppression, and what once was intrigue was now loathing.

Jacob stood staring at it. He didn't want to go in there anymore, to be surrounded by his life's work. All it did was remind him of his mistake, knowing it had all been for nothing. It was too much. Now that Peter was gone, Jacob knew that he had to destroy everything he had spent his whole life creating.

He took a deep breath and stepped inside. The whole cabin stank. It always stank. It was a putrid stench of decomposition and chemicals. Jacob first went to the bathroom to urinate. As he did his business, he observed the glass shards of the broken medicine cabinet on the floor. He knew that Peter had destroyed the medical cabinet; he had been down in the cellar when he had heard it.

Jacob finished his business and zipped up his pants. He stood in the living room and looked out the window at his Toyota, as well as the empty space next to it where the truck had been. Peter had the truck too, on top of everything else. Jacob had had two vehicles at the cabin: his own car and a truck he had rented to help transport bodies and equipment to the cabin. The fact that Peter stole the rental didn't do any favors for Jacob's anxiety. If Peter got pulled over or crashed, the rental company would surely investigate.

Jacob went into the bedroom and opened the filing cabinet next to his bed. There were numerous binders, dossiers and folders containing his research. He grabbed two armfuls and took them to the kitchen, where he placed them all neatly on the table. He planned to light the fireplace in the living room at some point and burn it all.

First things first, though; he needed to inspect the cellar. The subjects down there needed to be checked on.

For his entire life, Jacob had been unfazed by human anatomy. He'd seen countless cadavers in various stages of decomposition, fondled every organ, and performed surgery on living subjects. Yet now, looking at the ruins of his work in the cellar, he felt disgusted. The air was dense with death. Arms and hands were wired up to dials and chemical injections, heads bobbed in jars, and organs were hooked up to electrical equipment. All were decomposing now, and countless flies buzzed around as maggots crawled in and out of the limbs. The generators to the freezers had run out of gas, and even from afar Jacob could see their glass doors fog up with rotting condensation.

The Modern Prometheus

Jacob pressed his hand to his mouth, but thankfully his Eggs Benedict and coffee didn't come up. He regained his composure, lifted his shirt to his mouth and walked over to one of the freezers.

It was like everything in his mind had changed, ever since Peter was born. No longer did he look at these human parts as scientific subjects, but rather for what they really were: *human*.

Was this how a parent felt? Upon birthing a child, new fears and emotions emerge that had never been there before. Peter's birth had unearthed a part of reality that Jacob had either deliberately ignored or was completely unaware of. It was the most horrible and frightening thing about this whole ordeal: how ignorant he had been.

How could it all have come to this? he thought, pressing his hand on the glass of the freezer. *How could I have allowed my life to become this? To do all this?*

All this—his work, his crippling fear of death, and his obsession with the preservation of life—began, whether he wanted it to or not, when he was a nine-year-old boy on a skiing trip with his parents.

Jacob had never been close to his parents. He had never even really had a family—no sisters or brothers, and while he was aware of his aunts and uncles, he never met them. His parents were aloof and caught up in their own work. His father,

Brian, was a respected surgeon at the University of Medicine in Chicago. His mother, Edie, was a professor of molecular biology at Johns Hopkins. Despite being married for ten years before Jacob was even born, Brian and Edie didn't have much of a relationship either. They lived seven hundred miles away from each other—Brian in Chicago and Edie in Baltimore. Not even Jacob knew why they got married or even had a child. Both were married to their professions.

Jacob was raised in Chicago, in a big house in the Loop, and was taken care of and schooled by a hired nanny, an older woman named Marleney Portela. While Marleney was a sweet woman, and provided as much as she could, she wasn't a parent and couldn't provide the love that Jacob needed.

Jacob grew up reading his parents' medical and scientific textbooks because there was nothing else in the house to do. No television, no games, no love. Everything in the house was cold—art was an alien concept to the Abbott family, and there were no paintings or sculptures around. Everything was science.

Every couple of months, Brian and Edie would meet in Chicago to play family for a week before they went their separate ways again. The skiing trip that changed Jacob's life had been on one of those occasions. Brian and Edie took Jacob to Gore Mountain in North Creek, New York. Never had Jacob skied before, and never would he ski again afterwards.

Dressed in their windbreaker suits and boots secured with skis, the Abbott family went up and down the mountain all day. Skiing, as it turned out, had come naturally to Jacob. He had struggled at first, but after his fourth trip down the mountain, he had become entirely comfortable with his movement and momentum.

It was towards the end of the afternoon when it happened. After the Abbott family ascended the mountain for perhaps the eighth time, Jacob felt a little cocky. He sped ahead of his parents, zipping down the trail, with his ski poles tucked under his arms. Then, he hit a patch of ice. The front of his left ski stuck into the ground, and Jacob went soaring face first into the snow. The impact knocked him unconscious.

Three days passed before Jacob finally woke up. He was in Lennox Hospital in New York City, having been airlifted there after the tumble. Jacob's spleen had ruptured in the accident, and he needed immediate medical attention. A little past midnight on November 7, 2000, nine-year-old Jacob Abbott became clinically dead for thirty-seven seconds before being resuscitated. Doctors had successfully removed his spleen and stabilized him.

Brian and Edie had deliberately kept this information from Jacob—who had assumed that he just had a nasty accident—until he was a teenager. It was his father who told him, because he felt "It was about time that you knew exactly what happened to you."

This revelation was traumatic to Jacob. Not at first—he was initially in disbelief over it, and even joked about it a few times with friends at school. But at night, as he lay in bed thinking it over, the knowledge of what had happened to him terrified him. He had been dead. He could have been *permanently* dead. But by some chance, he was alive. Ever since that revelation, he had developed a deep fear of death. He couldn't even watch movies where characters died. He didn't feel safe anywhere anymore.

Yet, he had also developed an obsession with death—to understand all its nuances and why it had to happen. When he was fifteen, he decided to devote his entire life to conquering the secrets of mortality. While he didn't explicitly tell his parents this, he did tell them that he wanted to enter medical school and become a doctor. This had delighted them to no end, and they spent whatever money was necessary for him to get the best education, training, and tutoring. They even gave him extra money to help him after he completed school. No expense was spared.

Mom, Dad, Jacob thought sadly as he stared at that freezer. *Would you be disappointed in me if you saw what I've done? With all your support, money, and expectations?*

The Modern Prometheus

In truth, Jacob had drifted away from his parents since he had gotten his doctorate. He wound up moving to Washington, D.C., where he lived as an on-campus resident at George Washington University School of Medicine. It was there, in his little flat, that he began his research that led to Peter Murphy's creation. There was plenty of money to begin work on this vision, from his parents, a few grants from the school, and loans.

The last time he had heard from his parents was when they sent him a Happy Birthday e-mail three years ago, but not since. In many ways, Jacob had become a lot like them: devoted to work, more than anything else. His parents had ensured that the path to his future was financially secured, and then all three had gone their separate ways.

The subjects—they had to be dealt with first. The paperwork he could burn last, but these bodies had to go immediately. They were rotting faster than Jacob had anticipated. The summer heat was making it all the worse.

There was a suitcase upstairs that he could probably fill with some parts, weigh down with rocks, and then pitch somewhere. Mirror Lake was nearby, but there were too many vacation homes around it. The Pemigewasset River was also close, so that was an option too. Once he'd taken care of the bodies, then he could burn his research. After that, he would scrub the cabin top to bottom, leaving no trace that he was ever here.

26.

Just as Jacob was about to begin the dismal task of opening the freezer and removing the body parts, footsteps sounded above him. The wooden floor creaked as somebody moved through the living room and into the kitchen.

Jacob's mouth went dry. He knew immediately who it was, because he had been expecting Peter to return. He grabbed a dirty scalpel from the table next to him and slowly crept up the staircase. He was determined to not allow Peter to get away again.

Through the doorway, Jacob could see the kitchen. There he sat, wearing a dirty white T-shirt, jeans and sunglasses at the table, thumbing through a file. It looked like Peter's shirt was stained with small spots of blood—not an excessive amount, but enough to notice.

"Peter," Jacob said hoarsely.

Peter looked up from the file. He set it on the table and stood from his chair. "You were expecting me," he said, gesturing with a nod at the scalpel.

Meekly, Jacob stepped through the doorway and lowered the scalpel. This was the first time he was getting a good look at his creation since the night of the escape, and already he was noticing alarming red flags. There were red patches all over

Peter's arms and face, like irritated sunburns or rashes. It looked like the skin around those red spots was peeling.

"I guess I was," Jacob said.

"I'm not here to kill you, though I probably should." Peter scratched at a rash on his arm. "What did you do to me?"

This was a question that Jacob had never anticipated being confronted with. He should have, but he hadn't. In truth, he had never even thought that he would make it this far.

"I uh… didn't think my research would be a success."

Peter's eyebrows rose. "This is what you'd refer to as a 'success'?"

"No, I just—"

"What did you do to me? Answer me!"

"Sit back down, Peter. I'll start at the beginning."

Peter sat. He didn't take his gaze off Jacob, and his eyes were visible through those dark lenses, full of ferocity and pain. Jacob sat across from him at the table but found it difficult to look directly into Peter's face. It was lifelike, but also not. It dipped into the uncanny valley. His creation had all the physical characteristics of a human but lacked the subtleties that would otherwise be recognizable in our species.

Peter leaned forward and cupped his hands together. Now that he was closer, Jacob could see the rashes on his creation's face and arms more clearly. The irritated spots in his skin were covered with scratch marks, like Peter had been itching himself feverishly.

"You gonna say anything?" Peter said, his hands tightening together on the table.

This was the most awkward situation Jacob had ever been in. It was almost comical, like being on some late-night TV sitcom. He tried to figure out the best way to approach this, but he then concluded that there was no easy way to tell the truth.

"I've been—I've," he stammered. *What should I say?* "I've been researching a project of great interest to me."

"That project being me, I take it."

"You are the result of many years devoted to science."

"I'll be very direct with you, Jacob. I don't give a shit about who you are or what your research is. All I know is that you're responsible for making me wake up"—he fluttered his hand—"in *this*."

"What do you already know, Peter?"

"I'm dead." He said this venomously, as if he resented saying it out loud. "I am dead, and my son is dead. My whole life is gone. My wife ran away from me. My brother refuses to acknowledge me. My co-workers and friends don't recognize me. I haven't seen my daughter yet, but I can only assume that if she sees me, then that won't end well either. My family, my career, my own fucking body is gone. Everything that was Peter Murphy has ceased to exist!"

So, he did try to go back to his family, Jacob thought.

"I don't know how you did this, Jacob, but I want an explanation now."

Jacob swallowed. "It was a car accident, Peter. It happened six months ago, in December. The crash killed both you and your son. I don't know many details about it. Frankly, I didn't need to know anything else besides the damage done to your body, and how I could work around it."

"And you brought me back?"

"Yes."

"But not Jack?"

"No, I—I was afraid to work on a child."

"Because you understood what would happen."

"Two reasons. Your bodies were badly damaged in the accident, and parts of you needed to be replaced. None of the parts that I had would suit a child as young as Jack. The other reason is that I had no way to access your son's body."

"You've been harvesting dead bodies?"

"Yes. First, two cadavers from the university I was living at. I got paranoid and stopped, because I believed campus security was suspicious of me. After I came here to New Hampshire, I began acquiring subjects from a funeral director in your town."

"The funeral director that worked on me and Jack?"

"Your will stated that you wanted to be cremated, while Jack was to have a traditional burial. The funeral director informed me of your upcoming cremation. I picked your body up and he filled the urn selected by your family with the ashes of an unclaimed body. I offered him a generous sum of money from my research grant. The ashes of that unclaimed body are buried with your son. The funeral director helped me acquire four subjects total, including yours.

"There were two experiments before you, Peter. They were failures. I became desperate, working against time, because decomposition was threatening my work. When I got to you, I had to replace parts of your body with parts from other subjects, either because of the damage in your accident or general necrosis."

"What parts are no longer me?" He pointed at his feminine hand. "Who is this?"

"Your body is made up of three different subjects, Peter. The primary one is Peter Murphy. The other two are a Caucasian woman and an African American man."

Jacob reached across the table and pushed away a few folders until he found a green binder. He flipped through its laminated pages until he found a photo of a woman in her late thirties with short hair, thin lips, and a sharp nose. She held a

German Shepherd and sat near a lake, smiling brightly for the camera. Jacob turned the binder around and pushed it across the table for Peter to see.

"This is Angela Fairhardt. She was a mother of two who lived in West Warwick, Rhode Island. She died of a seizure back in January, when she was only thirty-eight years old. She was epileptic. She was to be cremated and buried in Atkinson, where she grew up. I acquired her body from the funeral home. You have her hand, her heart, and a few of her bones. Turn over to the next page."

Peter did so. A photo of a young African American man sitting on a couch with a modest, bashful smile appeared. A woman—possibly his girlfriend—sat next to him, with her arms around him and her face pressed against his.

"That is Timothy Saunders of Lowell, Massachusetts," Jacob explained. "He was a maintenance worker and passed away at twenty-seven from an accidental mixture of sleeping pills and pain medication in February. I guess he was suffering from pneumonia, sleeping problems, and had bad joint pain. Mixing the medications caused cardiac arrest in his sleep. I acquired his body from the same funeral home. You have Timothy's foot, leg, one of his eyes, one of his lungs, his liver, and his jaw."

Peter pressed his hand against his chin and rubbed it. He ran his tongue against the backs of his teeth on the bottom row. Now he understood why they didn't feel right.

"You sick son of a bitch. What gives you the right to fuck with peoples' lives like this?" Peter stood and slapped his hands against the table. "I did not consent to this. Do you understand? I did not ask for this body, for this life! I am an affront to God! *I DO NOT CONSENT TO THIS!*"

"You want revenge, Peter?"

"I said that I'm not here to kill you." Peter straightened his posture, with his chest out and his shoulders flat, commandeering the direction of the conversation. "Listen, how you made this possible means nothing to me. I don't care how much money you spent, or how hard you worked, or any of that. You've committed an injustice against me, and for that you owe me something."

"What are you saying?"

"My son. You're going to bring him back to me."

"You were just talking about how I've committed a great injustice by bringing you back, and now you want me to do the same to your son?"

"Two and a half years old. He was only two and a half fucking years old! Robbed from this world. My life and everything I've done with it is gone, but Jack? He never even had a chance."

"Even if I did bring him back, the world would reject him just as it has with you."

"He would have *me!*" Now Peter sounded as if he were pleading. "Jack would still have me. I could raise him—I would still be able to give him a life he never got to have."

"It's not possible, Peter."

Peter scowled, lifted the front of his shirt and drew a gun from his pants. He circled around the table, grabbed Jacob by the hair, and pointed the gun between his eyes.

"If you can't bring my son back, then you're worthless to me."

All at once that terror—that great mortal dread that had followed Jacob throughout his life—came rushing into his heart. He threw his arms out and made panicked squeaks.

"Yeah, it's fucking scary, isn't it?" Peter taunted. "Death is scary! How about I kill you, then bring you back and throw you to the fucking wolves!"

"Six months!"

"What?"

"Six—months!"

Peter let go and stepped back. "You have about five seconds to explain yourself."

Jacob ran his fingers through his hair. It took him a moment to compose himself after having a gun pointed at his face. Once his mortal dread was tamed, Jacob explained: "Jack has been dead for six months. The funeral director filled his body with embalming fluid, but this only temporarily slows decomposition to make viewings possible. It does not stop decomposition. After six months, all the flesh and organs of your son—it's just not possible. He's practically slime and bones by this point."

Peter's brow went flat. Jacob could see how crushed his creation had become by this information. Peter's hand wielding the gun trembled and his chin quivered. He slipped the gun back into the front of his pants and pressed Angela's hand against his mouth.

"For a moment, I believed I could be with him again," Peter said faintly.

"I'm sorry, Peter. It can't happen. Your son is gone."

"I never got to teach him how to drive. I never got to see him graduate from college, or get married, or *anything*." His voice choked, and he turned to the window. For a long time, he looked outside. "He was only two and a half. Still a baby."

"Peter, the only reason why I could bring you back is because your body was still fresh. Your cadaver was kept in a freezer—first at the county medical examiner, then at the funeral home. I've set up a few freezers here in the cabin that I bought, and they've kept you preserved as well. Whatever parts of you that were decomposed, I was able to replace with parts from other preserved bodies. I just can't do anything with a body that has been decomposing for that long."

The grief receded. Peter turned away from the window and stared at the doctor, his eyes alight with inspiration. "Only with fresh bodies?" he uttered.

"There are a few other variables to consider, but generally I need fresh subjects, yes."

Peter turned back to the window, staring at the forest outside. He began scratching at a rash on his neck, dragging his nails across it until it bled. Peter pulled his hand back, examined the blood on his fingertips and then wiped them against his shirt.

"You told me that the police were after me," Peter said. "Is that true? Why?"

An uncomfortable look crossed Jacob's face. "I lied."

"You lied? Excuse me?"

"I'm sorry, Peter. I was afraid that you might try and leave. I couldn't have the world find out about you. I needed to lie to keep you here."

"Would I not leave anyway? Were you just planning on keeping me here forever?"

"I had… ideas." Jacob knew that there was no way to defend anything he had done. "I didn't think I would get this far. All my thoughts were committed to just making the experiment work—making *you* work. I didn't consider much after that. I had ideas, though. I thought that maybe… I could help you. I could get a house out in the country, take you with me, and—"

"Study me?" Peter interjected. "Is that right? Keep me alone somewhere in the middle of nowhere so that you can run tests on me? Document how I respond to medications or my environment? Keep me part of your fucking science experiment as a guinea pig?"

Jacob's face was stoic, but there was shame in his eyes. It tried to hide, but it was there. "I take responsibility," he finally said.

"Oh you'll take responsibility, all right." Peter licked his lips. "Before I escaped, you tried to kill me. You filled a syringe with something. You said it was medicine, but I knew from the look on your face that it wasn't. I know that you intended to kill me. Why?"

"Peter, when I brought you back, I was blinded by my own achievements. It was only when…"

"Only what?"

"It was only when you began talking about your family that I realized I may have made a mistake. You retained all of your memories. I don't know why I didn't think of it. Maybe because I didn't want to think about it, because it would have slowed me down. You remembered who you were. You remembered your wife and children. I didn't just create a life out of thin air from parts of the dead. I brought back a man who had lived and then died. Your essence preceded your existence."

"My essence?"

"Jean-Paul Sartre. He believed that humans are born into the world without a distinct purpose. Purpose is essence. Tools have their essence preceded by their existence because they are created with a specific purpose. Everything about their physical characteristics is crafted for that purpose."

Jacob drew a pen from his pocket and held it up for Peter to see. "Take this pen, for example. This pen exists because people need to write or draw. As such, there is a reason for this pen to exist, and everything about its characteristics—the ink, the tip, the little button on the bottom—all serve to make that possible. As such, the purpose of this pen—its *essence*—precedes its existence, giving it a reason to be here. Its essence is a blueprint for its existence." He slipped the pen back into his pocket. "Do you understand what I'm trying to say?"

"Philosophy wasn't one of my departments, but I understand the basics."

"Humans are abstract and find their essence after they are born—their existence precedes their essence, in other words. We are brought into this world, we learn who we are, how we function, what we like, and we try to find purpose for why we were born based on those characteristics. Before you died, you created essence by starting a family and establishing a career. After you died and I brought you back, that essence had preceded your current existence. You were born and created a life for yourself, but then that life you created is gone. Now, you have been brought back, and without that essence, you merely exist. You are purposeless. I don't know how you could create your own essence now."

"Then what the hell was I to you?"

"I saw you as a tool, Peter. Except I didn't create you to serve any specific purpose other than to validate my own fears and ego. That was my greatest insult to you and to nature. You were a human being."

"I don't feel human anymore," Peter said bitterly. "I am not natural. I was not born or conceived naturally. Who are you to say what is human and what isn't anymore? You have raped the laws of this Earth."

"Peter—"

"Another thing! Look at this." He gestured at the rashes on his face and arms. "What is going on with my skin? It's so itchy that it's driving me insane."

Jacob pursed his lips and did not answer.

"Well?" Peter pressed.

"I think you're merely shedding skin, Peter. Your body is very weak. Everything about it is weak—your organs, your muscles, your ligaments—and you've been putting it under a lot of emotional and physical stress. You have been exerting a lot of energy, running and driving around, trying to talk to people, suffering emotional duress. I don't think your body can handle it all. You need to rest, Peter. Give your body a break."

"You're saying these are stress rashes? I've never once had stress rashes before."

"You've also never experienced reanimation, and all the consequences that accompany it. I'd say that's pretty stressful."

Peter sat back and squinted at the doctor. He had a point. "And this is normal? I have no reason to be afraid?"

"I would prefer it if you stay with me, so that I can run a few tests on you."

Peter laughed. "I'm not doing that. I don't want you putting your disgusting hands on me again—never again. All I need is the reassurance is that I'll be fine."

Again, Jacob took several moments to answer, then said, "You'll be fine, Peter. So long as you take a few days to just *rest*, you'll be okay."

"That's not all, either. Yesterday, I had some sort of memory lapse episode. I suddenly lost my train of thought, and then I completely forgot who I was, where I was, and what I was doing. It lasted for probably a few moments, but it scared the hell out of me."

"Has this happened more than once?"

"No, just that one time, but… I feel off. I get confused a lot, and sometimes I feel and think in ways I can't explain. It doesn't feel like me. I know how I would respond to things, and how I've been dealing with everything… it's just not characteristic of me." Peter shrugged. "Then again, I don't know how else I can respond to what's happened to me."

"I think the lapses in memory can be easily explained, Peter. I don't think you're going to like it, though."

"Just say it."

"It may be related to severe emotional and psychological trauma. You've suffered a great deal in such a short span of time. You woke up here, with parts of your body missing or replaced, alone and frightened. Then you escaped, and once you finally got home, you discovered that you and your son are dead. Then your wife rejected you, as did your own brother and colleagues.

The Modern Prometheus

And now you're being presented with the truth of what happened to you. This is a lot to process in such a small span of time, Peter. The memory lapses and mental cloudiness might be related to something akin to post-traumatic stress disorder."

Peter looked ill. "I don't know how to respond to that."

"Please keep in mind, I am not a psychologist, so I'm not officially diagnosing you, but I think it is a possibility to consider. You may feel hyper-vigilant, maybe even aggressive, and you might have intrusive thoughts or feelings."

"I'm going to be sick."

"That's okay, Peter. You don't—"

"Don't try to console me! You did this to me. I don't need your sympathy."

"I am your caregiver, Peter."

"You are no such thing!" Peter pointed at him. "I don't want anything from you right now, do you understand? I just want to be left alone!"

"Okay, Peter. That's fair. I can leave you alone."

"Do you have a cell phone?"

"Huh?"

"I said, do you have a cell phone?"

"I don't."

"You're living in the third decade of the twenty-first century and you don't have a cell phone? You brought a dead man back to life, but *you don't have a fucking cell phone?*"

"I'm paranoid, Peter. Cell phones, they're filled with all these tracking devices. I can't have anyone know what I've been doing here."

"Fine. A phone of any kind?"

"There's a landline."

"Give me the number."

Jacob took a sheet of paper from one of the folders and went into the living room. There was a phone on the end table next to the couch. The number was inscribed on a sticker underneath it. Jacob scribbled the number on the paper and handed it to Peter.

"I'll be in touch," Peter said.

"Where are you going?"

"None of your business." Peter grabbed several folders and binders off the table and stuffed them under his arm.

"Hey!" Jacob grabbed a folder from Peter. "You can't take these!"

"These were the instruments of my creation. I'm taking them."

"They need to be destroyed!"

Peter drew the pistol from his pants again. "I am taking some of your research, Jacob. If you want to destroy it, fine. But I'm taking some of it. Especially this." He took up the green binder containing the files on Angela Fairhardt and Timothy Saunders. "I have some research of my own to do."

"What are you going to do?"

"I told you that's none of your goddamned business!" Peter took one last folder and added it to the stack under his arm. "I need to be alone for a while. I'll call you. Make sure that you stay with that phone."

Jacob saw the bleeding rash on Peter's neck. Another driblet of blood rolled down his throat and stained the collar of his shirt.

"Wait a minute, Peter."

"What is it now?"

"Your rashes. The one on your neck is bleeding."

"I don't care."

"I don't think—"

"I said that I don't want to hear it! Do you understand? I have a lot on my mind right now. If I hear anything else, then I'm going to lose my fucking mind. I just can't take it anymore."

Without arguing, Jacob passed Peter and entered the bathroom. He grabbed a roll of gauze from the destroyed medicine cabinet and returned to the kitchen.

"At least take this." He handed Peter the gauze. "You can't do much when you're bleeding all over the place."

Peter eyed the gauze, and then stuffed it into his pocket. "Don't miss a call from me."

"Peter, listen... I know that you don't want anything from me, but if you need something, anything at all, please let me know."

"Just give me a few days. That's all. Just give me time to be alone and think, then I'll contact you."

With the binders and folders under his arm, Peter stepped out of the kitchen, passed through the living room, and went out the front door. Through the window, Jacob watched his creation get into the rental truck and drive away, vanishing in the forest.

27.

This situation was way worse than Jacob could have possibly imagined. He anxiously paced from one end of the cabin to the other, feeling sweat under his arms and the middle of his back. This was bad. This was potentially *catastrophic*.

Peter wasn't just a creation with the memories and emotions of a man who was dead, but he now possessed *intent*. What that intent was, Jacob wasn't entirely sure, but Peter needed some of his research for a reason. None of this boded well. It also wasn't assuring that Peter now had a gun. Where did he get it? His house? Would he really hurt someone? Peter seemed more liable to hurt himself than anyone else.

Give him time, Jacob thought. *All of this has been overwhelming to him. Maybe he's right. Maybe he just needs space. It's not like being resurrected is a common occurrence, unless you happen to be a biblical figure. He* did *say that he would be in touch.*

Maybe Jacob could reason with Peter once he calmed down and organized his thoughts. Maybe this didn't have to end tragically. He just needed to be patient.

You wanted to kill him the moment you realized that you had made a mistake, and now you want to try and reason with him?

It seemed like a contradiction, but Jacob's compromise stemmed from the fact that he was no longer in control over the situation. He had wanted to kill Peter, but that had been when he was still under Jacob's control—before he knew what had happened to him and what he became. Now that that line had already been crossed, Jacob might as well try to sway the circumstances into his favor.

Jacob sat down at the table, drummed his fingers against it and wiped sweat from his forehead.

"*Study me? Is that right?*"

It was true. Jacob had wanted to keep Peter to himself. He had wanted to study him and see just how far he could take him as an experiment. Yet, was that the only reason? Or was it also because Jacob was afraid of being alone in this world? He had spent his entire life alone, after all. Absent parents, no relatives, no friends, no lovers. Nothing.

Now that he was mulling over it, Jacob realized that he had dreamed often about living with his creation once he was successfully reanimated—teaching him things, taking care of him, and most of all, having someone to talk to. It was a fantasy that had made him feel less lonely, and as much as Jacob hated to admit it, it was one of the things that drove him to work as hard as he did to succeed.

Could this truly not end tragically?

Jacob thought about those horrible rashes all over Peter's body. Some of them even looked infected. He also considered the memory loss episode that Peter had described. Jacob wasn't sure exactly what was happening, but he had a grim theory.

It *was* possible that the rashes were caused by stress, and the memory loss and confusion episodes *could* be from emotional trauma, but Jacob feared something else as well. He had just been afraid to tell Peter the full truth of what he believed was happening to him.

The human body constantly sheds dead cells and grows new ones to replace the dead ones. Such a process is ingrained in our DNA. There was a period of time after Peter was reborn when his body began an aggressive re-growth of new cells. While he was drifting in and out of consciousness for a few weeks following his rebirth, several layers of Peter's skin had shed and scabbed over as new living cells replaced the dead cells. Peter even had vomiting and diarrhea episodes as his organs healed and began functioning again. His body eventually recovered, and everything seemed normal after that.

However, it now looked as if Peter's body had stopped reproducing new cells to replace the dead ones. Either that or the cells in his body were rapidly dying off altogether, faster than new ones could be produced. Why this was happening, Jacob couldn't be completely sure. It was possible that some unforeseen corruption had occurred in Peter's body or DNA during the process of his creation. Stress may be a contributing factor, but Jacob knew that those rashes looked much worse than mere stress rashes.

This was why Peter's skin was starting to chap and rash over. It would bleed and never heal. This wasn't just limited to the skin, but would affect the organs and muscles as well. Maybe a week or a month from now—there was no realistic time frame Jacob could predict—Peter will die. It will be a slow and agonizing death from organ failure, shock, blood loss, or countless other possibilities.

To make matters worse, this also meant that Peter's brain was rotting away as well. There was no telling how this would affect him psychologically or emotionally. This was why the memory loss alarmed Jacob.

While Peter may be suffering from post-traumatic stress disorder, his mental health was possibly further jeopardized by the fact that the cells in his brain—including the nerve cells—were dying off. This would cause adverse physical and chemical alterations in his brain. Any number of symptoms were on the table: memory loss, irritability, confusion, personality changes, lack of restraint, seizures, and he could even begin suffering from hallucinations. The list just went on and on. Peter could go senile, or even insane—if he didn't suffer a serious seizure and die first.

When Jacob had handed Peter the gauze, he had considered telling him all this, but held back. Why hadn't he said anything? Was it because he wanted Peter to die, to have his suffering end? Was it because he had been afraid that Peter would be driven over the edge if he knew the full scope of what was happening to him?

Or maybe it was because Jacob didn't have the heart to tell a man he had brought back from the dead that he was losing his mind and decomposing to death.

28.

The town of Salem straddles the Massachusetts border, nestled between the cities of Methuen and Haverhill, and the towns of Atkinson and Pelham. It is a commercial town, referred to as the "Gateway to New Hampshire" for people coming in from the Bay State. Along with neighborhoods, the town is home to a wide variety of restaurants, shopping districts, and hotels.

It was in this town that Peter decided to set up his base of operations. It was directly next to Atkinson, and about a half-hour drive from Manchester, where he knew his daughter was and where he suspected his wife to be.

Near Exit 2 off I-93 was a cheap motel with rickety steel walkways, dirty windows and a parking lot littered with trash. A sign greeted Peter as he pulled in that read "Rockingham Motel."

The woman at the front desk gave him disconcerting looks as he rented a room, but her general attitude was that she was used to funny-looking people. Peter got a room for three nights, paying two hundred dollars. The woman didn't argue—didn't seem to care either. Peter used his wife's debit card. He had gone to the ATM in the lobby prior to speaking to the woman at the desk and saw that Margie had plenty of money in her checking account. The money was likely from Peter's life insurance. It would be enough.

Room 205 was predictably dreary. The bed sheets were dirty and covered in hair, and the carpet stank of machine oil. A wooden desk and chair sat in one corner of the room, and a shanty TV on a steel stand sat in another. That was it. It was more than Peter needed. All he wanted was privacy, and for nobody to know where he was.

The first thing Peter did was set all the folders and binders on the table, and then plugged the charger into the outlet next to the bed to charge his wife's phone. After that, he grabbed the alarm clock from the bedside table, then went into the bathroom and smashed the mirror over the sink with it. Once that was taken care of, he sat on the edge of the grimy bed and caressed his face. He could feel the skin peeling, and it burned to the touch. More spots were bleeding on his cheek and forehead.

This awful rash started shortly after he left his brother's place the night before, first emerging on his arm, then spreading to other parts of his body soon after. By the time he reached the cabin, his whole body was itchy.

Whatever, he thought. *Jacob will fix it. If he can bring a man back to life, then he should be able to figure this out and get it fixed. But that can come later.*

Another voice in his mind interjected, *Are you just telling yourself that because you don't want to think about it? Because you're afraid?*

There was some truth to that. At the same time, part of Peter hoped that there was something wrong with him. It wasn't like he wanted to continue like this, existing the way he did now. He had, after all, nearly shot himself not long ago. If he was going to die, then he wanted to at the very least use whatever time he had left to do something proactive—something he wouldn't be able to do had he not returned from the grave. Regardless of what the problem was, it only pressured him to keep moving. *Distractions. I can't allow myself to get distracted.*

The first thing he needed to do, above all else, was take care of his body. If something was wrong with it, then the least that he could do was take a shower, just in case he was at risk for any infections.

Peter went into the bathroom. He took a few moments to prepare himself before he undressed, and when he did, he stood naked looking down at his ruined body. The stitching along his abdomen and chest was something he had actively avoided thinking about, but now he decided that it was the time to really examine it. The incisions themselves looked as if they had healed, but the stitching remained. Peter picked at the stitches, and they hurt to the touch.

The rashes covered his entire body now. The worst areas seemed to be under his arms, his groin area, and his lower abdomen. A shower would be good. It would be healthy.

Peter turned the shower on and waited for the water to get hot, and then stepped in.

It felt good. All the sweat and grime that had been accumulating on his body since he had escaped the cabin washed off. The water on the floor of the tub turned black and green. Peter closed his eyes, relishing the sensation of the hot water.

He began running his fingers through his hair, and then scrubbed his scalp with his fingernails. Thick flakes of dandruff peeled off, and just as he was feeling relaxed, a few fingernails on his right hand suddenly snapped off.

"Ack!" Peter took his hand out of his hair and examined his fingertips. The middle and ring finger nails had snapped off almost at the skin. The water stung the exposed flesh. Queasily, Peter pecked at his hair with his other hand until he found both fingernails tangled up in there. He pulled them out and dropped them into the tub.

Peter pointed out his index finger and began squeezing the tip of it. The nail on it popped right off.

Stress rashes. He scoffed. *These are NOT STRESS RASHES.*

Once again, Jacob had lied to him. Was there anything that fucking doctor told him true? There was no way to know for sure, and it only made Peter more paranoid. Nothing and nobody could be trusted, not even his own damn body.

Peter shut the shower off, quickly got out of the tub, and dried himself off with a towel hanging on the door. By then his fingertips had stopped bleeding, but they stung.

I gotta patch myself up, he thought, getting back into his dirty clothes.

Peter dug out the gauze that Jacob had given him from his pocket. Carefully, he wrapped it around his head, starting at the neck. He looped it around his chin, mouth, nose, then finally his eyes and forehead. He was careful to make sure the bandages didn't limit his vision or breathing too badly, and once he finished, he slipped the sunglasses back on. They were a little wobbly on his face since his ears were covered, but the thickness of the bandages gave the nose pads enough grip to keep them secure. He then used what little was left of the gauze to wrap up his three exposed fingertips.

Time to get to work.

Peter returned to the main room, grabbed a few folders and binders, then spread them out on the table and began going through them. Most of it was busywork, such as approvals for grants and loans, mathematical equations, and scientific jargon. He looked at the files on Angela Fairhardt and Timothy Saunders, read them over, and set their photos down on the bed next to each other. It seemed Jacob had handwritten the files himself, and only covered basic information.

Angela reminded Peter of his own mother. It was the way she smiled, and the knowledge that she had two boys of her own. According to her file, she had been a cafeteria lady at Nathan Greene Middle School in Providence. Christian and Dale were the names of her children. She got divorced in 2010 and had full custody of the kids.

Peter picked her photo up. Thirty-eight years old, only a year older than Peter had been when he died. What had she been like? What had been her fears and anxieties? What had been the happiest day of her life? He wondered where her children were, and what had happened to their father.

Peter held his hand up next to the photo—this hand that had once belonged to Angela. He examined her hand in the photo, and then examined her hand on his wrist. He twiddled Angela's fingers in front of his face, examining the tendons through the skin.

You're part of me now, Angela, he thought.

Next, he took up the photo of Timothy Saunders. He had been enrolled at the University of Massachusetts studying mechanical engineering. As a child he had loved rocket ships and wanted to be an astronaut when he grew up. His girlfriend's name was Regina, and together they had a little girl named Ruby.

Regina was a nurse at Holy Family Hospital, and they had moved to Atkinson only two years ago so that they could provide a quiet life for their baby.

Peter pulled up his pant leg and considered Timothy's leg. He stretched out his toes and examined the spaces between them. *You're part of me too, Tim,* Peter thought. *I guess we're all one big happy family in one body, aren't we?*

The last file in the binder was on Peter, detailing his education, childhood, and family. Curiously, Peter flipped through the paperwork on himself, but stopped when he saw a photo attached near the back.

The photo was of Peter dead, lying on one of the porcelain slabs in the cellar of the cabin. Two incisions went up the sides of his head, and his face was pulled up over his scalp, exposing his red skull. Timothy Saunders's jaw was wired to it. Peter scowled at this photo for several seconds, and then shut the binder and threw it across the room.

I didn't need to see that, he thought. *No, that was the last thing I ever wanted to see.*

He covered his eyes with his palms. What he had just seen burned into his mind. He had looked like meat in a slaughterhouse—*that had been him.*

"For Christ's"—he belched sickly.

To repel the memory, Peter quickly took up a folder and began flipping through it. If he just kept reading, eventually what he had seen would settle into the back of his mind, rather than in the front.

He suddenly heard his wife's phone vibrating on the bed. He looked over and saw its screen glowing. He got up and picked the phone up. Owen was calling.

Peter's brow furrowed. For a moment his thumb hovered over the answer button, but it did not commit. He set the phone back down on the bed and returned to the table. It was best not to answer. It would only complicate things.

As he continued flipping through the folder, he discovered a stack of papers, stapled together from the medical examiner, containing the autopsy reports for Peter and Jack Murphy. Peter hesitated to look through them, but then decided that he needed to know the full scale of what had happened to him and his son.

The engine of the car had burst through the dashboard and the roof had caved in. Peter's chest had been crushed, snapping several ribs, two of which had pierced his left lung. He had drowned in his own blood. Along with this, his hand and leg had been mangled.

Jack's death, however, had been far more gruesome. When the engine block burst through the dashboard, Jack had been in his booster seat on the passenger side. The engine had pulverized his skull into pieces and killed him instantly.

Peter set the file down and stared blankly ahead. He kept imagining the crash that night. He couldn't remember any of it, but he suspected that he did somewhere in his subconscious. He could imagine himself in his car, gurgling blood, and looking over to see the engine pinned into Jack's booster seat, with pieces of his skull—

Don't even think about it, Peter thought. *No, I can't think about it. It's too much.*

Peter flipped through the rest of the autopsy report. Stapled to the back was a police report, dated from the night he and his son had died.

ARREST REC: 12/22/20

OFFENDER: FRANKLIN DELAHUNTY

CHARGE: VEHICULAR MANSLAUGHTER

ARRESTING OFFR: TROOPER AMY NORRIS

NARRATIVE: At precisely 7:46 p.m. on December 22, 2020, Franklin "Frankie" Delahunty (19) of Methuen, Massachusetts, struck the vehicle of Peter K. Murphy (37) half a mile before Exit 2 of I-495. Delahunty was driving a 2007 Ford Explorer, which collided with Murphy's 2015 Chevrolet

Impala, killing both Murphy and his son John "Jack" Murphy (2). Delahunty received minor lacerations and a fractured left arm, and was treated at Holy Family Hospital under police supervision. Peter and John Murphy D.O.A. Investigation of the crash will be conducted on 12/24/20 by the Massachusetts State Police and the Highway Division. Delahunty is expected to be released on bail 12/23/20 by his mother, Cynthia Delahunty (42), with the aid of Massachusetts bail bond agent CRAIG FINNERTY of BOSTON CAPITAL BAIL BONDS. No further comment can be made.

Here were the answers to all his questions. Peter had always suspected it, but with the police and autopsy reports now in his hands, he knew that it was true. He didn't just die in a car accident. He was killed by someone else. *His son was killed by someone else.*

This teenage kid, Franklin Delahunty—this was his son's killer, and his address was in the police report: 55 Byron Street, Methuen, Massachusetts.

There wasn't any need to read further, so he slipped the report back into the folder. The metal of the pistol in his pants was cold against his itchy skin. He took it out and set it on the table, contemplating it as he ran his finger along it.

The Modern Prometheus

The name and address kept repeating in his head: *Franklin Delahunty. 55 Byron Street. Franklin Delahunty. 55 Byron Street.*

29.

In the morning, Peter woke up in a bed that he knew wasn't his, in a room that he knew wasn't his, with no recollection of how he got there or why. Immediately, he sat up, and his eyes darted all around this alien, squalid room.

"What?"

There were stacks of files and folders on a wooden table, a mirror was smashed in the bathroom, and when he touched his face, he felt the moist fabrics of bandages.

How did I get there? What's on my face?

Confusion clouded his mind, and he tore the sheets off himself, leapt out of the bed, and went to the door to escape, thinking he had gotten kidnapped. He stopped himself upon seeing a woman's hand stitched onto his arm as he reached out to grab the doorknob.

"What?" He grabbed his wrist, bewildered and shocked. "How—"

Angela. The name came to him like a bullet in that storm of confusion. *Angela… Fairman? Hart? FAIRHARDT.*

Slowly, his memories returned to him again. He pressed his fingertips against his temples. The inside of his head felt raw, like his brain was swollen. It was pulsating.

Right, I came here, he reminded himself. *After seeing Jacob... reading the police report... the shower—*

Franklin Delahunty.

Peter felt his pockets until he found the bottle of aspirin. He popped three into his mouth and began chewing them. He sat on the edge of the bed, the world slowly returning to him, recollecting everything.

The Delahunty kid, killed me and Jack, plans, plans, plans.

The swelling in his head felt like it was weakening, and his thoughts and memories slowly organized themselves. The haze of confusion cleared, like emerging from a fog. Peter began to feel normal again.

Normal, that's a word for it. He chuckled bitterly. *These memory lapses and confusion episodes are getting serious. I gotta get to work. My body is working against me.*

Peter got off the bed and stood before the window to look out at the parking lot. There were only a few ramshackle cars, trash piling up in the grass along the edges of the lot, and a lone custodian sweeping up cigarette butts near the check-in office.

There was no way to predict how everything would turn out, but he had a general idea. First though, he needed to see it for himself. There were things he needed to be certain about. It would be unpleasant not only because of his intentions, but because he wasn't particularly thrilled to see the residence of his murderer.

Before he considered anything else, though, he had to eat. The last time he ate was yesterday morning, back at his house, so by now he was starving. Where could he eat? The bandages all over his face and hands would draw attention, and if he was going to go through with what he intended, then he needed to keep a low profile. That meant no restaurants or grocery stores. Maybe a fast-food drive-through, but even that seemed shady.

Peter decided to look around the motel, so he stepped outside and took a walk. From what he could tell, besides the guy sweeping by the check-in office, there was nobody around. Regardless, he remained mindful of anyone who might be watching.

It was a hot day, and his sweat made the bandages sticky. He found a few vending machines behind the building. These would do. He got a few bags of chips, a soda, and some candy, and then returned to his room.

Breakfast of champions, he thought as he undid the bandages around his mouth and sat on the bed. He was ravenous. He wolfed down the chips and candy, and downed half of the soda in minutes. Once finished, he took a moment to digest.

Time to go, he thought.

Peter re-wrapped the bandages around his mouth and stood. As he went to grab the truck keys from the table, a sharp pain suddenly cut through his abdomen. He groaned and crossed his arms over his stomach. The nausea overwhelmed him.

"Good Christ."

He fell on his hands and knees and quickly undid the wrappings around his mouth again. Vomit erupted from his throat. Bright-red blood, undigested chips, and candy soaked the carpet. Peter stumbled onto his back away from the mess.

Another sharp pain came, and Peter prepared to vomit again, but nothing came out beyond a few gags and wheezes. Blood dripped from his lips, and he wiped them with the back of his hand.

I need—his thoughts stammered as he stared at the bloody mess on the carpet. *I need to get this done. What's happening to me must be worse than I thought. Get it done while I still have the nerve and time. Not to mention memory.*

Struggling, Peter got back on his feet, snatched the keys off the table and stepped out.

30.

The drive from Salem wasn't far, merely fifteen minutes. After taking I-93 down and navigating a few streets, Peter arrived.

The neighborhood was upper middle class, with sidewalks cutting through green knolls, old-fashioned wood and brick houses, and shrubbery separating each property. A couple jogged in their shorts and sweatbands, children threw around a basketball in the street, and an electrician climbed a telephone pole as another stood below on his radio.

Peter cruised in the truck from street to street until he reached Byron Street. He brought the vehicle to a crawling five miles per hour and eyed each house number until he spotted number fifty-five.

It was a sizable white house with brick foundations and steep gables. It was by no means a mansion, but it wasn't a shack, either. The residents of 55 Byron Street most certainly had money. A sprinkler was going, drizzling water all over the front yard, where a woman wearing a sunhat and khaki shorts stood with a weedwhacker, trimming the long grass under the front bushes. She was a middle aged woman, with grays in her dark hair and wrinkles around her mouth and eyes. At one point, she shut the weedwhacker off, took off the sunhat, and passed the back of her hand against her forehead. She then set the weedwhacker in the grass and took up a bottle of water from the stoop and drank from it.

Peter stopped the truck and focused on the woman. He was uncomfortable and paranoid. He didn't want anyone to notice a peculiar man with a bandaged face sitting in a truck by himself in the middle of a neighborhood. He was also frightened of getting confused again and forgetting why he was here. He kept the truck idling and lowered his seat back slightly, keeping his hand on the transmission handle and his foot on the brakes.

At one point, a chubby teenage kid wearing a cap and shorts with an unbuttoned shirt came up the sidewalk with a skateboard under his arm. The woman waved at the kid and sauntered over to meet him. They began chatting, and the woman nodded thumbed over her shoulder at the house.

Peter leaned forward. It was impossible to hear them, so he rolled down his window a crack, but this helped little. Their voices were muffled over the sound of a drill being used on the power lines up the street.

The woman smiled. She turned her head, held a hand to her mouth and hollered, "Frankie! Your friend is here!"

That's Cynthia Delahunty. It's gotta be, Peter thought.

Moments later, the front door opened, and a teenage kid stepped out. His hair was loose over his bright blue eyes, his nose was large and awkward, and he had a developing cleft chin. Like his friend, he had a skateboard under his arm.

Franklin went up to his friend and they began chatting. Cynthia took up the weedwhacker again and resumed her work.

Peter felt blood thumping dully in his ears. His eyes were set on that kid like a predator.

Franklin set his skateboard down on the sidewalk and placed a foot on it. His friend did the same and took off ahead of him. Just as Franklin hunched to propel himself forward, he turned his head, almost precisely, to look at where Peter was sitting in his truck. For one moment, Peter looked into the eyes of his murderer and the killer of his child.

Peter stomped on the gas and the truck sped down the street.

31.

The sun hung low against the horizon. The shadows of the headstones and statues of angels grew long against the freshly mowed grass. There were no other souls here to disturb him. Once again, Peter stood before the headstone that bore his name and the name of his son.

He stood piously, his hands folded in front of himself, and his head bowed. Occasionally, he cast his eyes at his mother's headstone to his left and sometimes wondered whether she would be ashamed of him.

There were many things on his mind. He kept thinking of Franklin Delahunty coming out of his house to greet his friend. It haunted him. To see the person who had robbed the world of his child drove his paternal instincts into overdrive. It was an offense of justice to see a child murderer smiling, talking with friends, free to do what he wanted.

Why was Franklin Delahunty free? The arrest report had mentioned that he had gotten off on bail. Did he have a future court date and trial? Would justice ever be served? It had been almost half a year since the crash. Would it really take that long? Had there been a miscarriage in the investigation and the whole thing got thrown out?

What if Franklin had gotten off on a light sentence, like community service and a hefty fine? Peter remembered once reading about a semi-truck driver in Mississippi who had driven through an intersection while on his phone, causing an accident that killed a thirty-year old woman. The truck driver had only been given sixty days jail time, Huber work-release privileges, and four years' probation on a charge of vehicular homicide by negligent operation of a vehicle.

Why? That was all Peter wanted to know. *Why* was Franklin not suffering in any way? Regardless of the degree of responsibility, Franklin Delahunty caused the death of his son, as well as Peter himself, and for that he must pay.

Am I capable of it?

Peter had always prided himself on being a man of academia, of reason and discourse. He had never been a violent person. The worst fight he had ever gotten into was when he had punched Mark Taberland in the back of the head in eleventh grade when Mark had harassed Owen. Even then Peter hadn't fought back when Mark's friends grabbed him and beat him down.

Then Peter remembered how he had grabbed Jacob Abbott by the hair, thrust the gun into his face and threatened to kill him. Peter had to fight to keep himself from pulling the trigger, and the only reason why he didn't was because at the time he had believed that Jacob could bring Jack back. Yet, in that moment, he felt he could have been capable of murder. He *wanted* to kill Jacob.

But I didn't kill him, Peter thought. *I don't have it in me. Do I?*

As he contemplated it, he recalled an experience one spring when Erin was probably no more than three years old. Peter had taken her to a big public park in Windham. There were basketball and tennis courts, an area to skateboard on half pipes, and a long, paved trail that went around the whole park for joggers. There was also a children's playground with monkey bars, swings, and a wooden fort with a slide.

Peter had been sitting on a wooden bench facing the play area, watching as Erin ran around with another little girl, going up ladders and climbing the jungle gym.

At one point, Peter had checked his phone. Margie had texted him saying that she was going to be late getting home and asked if Peter could take a few slices of meat out of the freezer to thaw when he returned. He had replied and slipped his phone back into his pocket, but upon raising his eyes back to the play area, he could no longer see Erin and her play friend. He stood, almost panicked, and circled the playground until he found her.

A man stood with her. He was balding, late middle aged, had a scraggly beard and wore ratty clothes with worn-out boots. He stood in front of Erin with his hands on his knees, whispering something to her.

Instantly, Peter charged over, grabbed Erin and pulled her away from the stranger.

"Hey man, it's cool. I just needed help with something," the man said.

This man's presence, demeanor, everything about him came off as threatening. Peter's hands had clenched into fists and he felt ready to attack him, but instead he shot a finger at the man. "Stay away from my daughter. From all these children."

The man backed away and sauntered toward the parking lot area. Peter watched him go until he was out of sight, then picked his daughter up and left the park. He never took Erin to that park again, not because he feared that any harm would come to her, but because he feared what he would do if he felt she was threatened like that again.

This memory came to Peter vividly. Was this violence he was now contemplating always there? Or did it only exist on some primitive, animalistic level, like a wolf assigned by nature to protect its cubs?

A few years back, Peter had read about a father in Louisiana who had shot and killed a man who had kidnapped his son. The kidnapper had taken the child to a motel in California, and he was only found when the boy managed to call his mother. The motel was raided, and the criminal was arrested and flown back to Louisiana. The father waited for him at Louis Armstrong International Airport, and as the kidnapper was escorted out of the terminal, the father emerged from the crowd and shot him in the head.

Few things in the world were as powerful as a father who would do anything to protect his children. *My children.* That was where Peter drew the line between being a reasonable man and being capable of harm. Regardless of the legal consequences Franklin may have faced or had yet to face, he had killed Peter's baby boy. That alone was enough to allow reason to slip away and to let Peter's own parental instincts take control of the wheel.

What do you have to lose? a voice intruded. *Just a few nights ago, you came close to blowing your brains out on this very grave. You only stopped because of your son. You might not be able to bring him back, but you yourself were brought back for a reason. Weren't you?*

But if I go through with this, I'll never have a chance to lead a normal life again.

You'll never be able to lead a normal life anyway, you imbecile. What makes you think that you can ever start over? It's hopeless. You do not exist. The world considers you dead and has moved on from you. What, are you just going to start a part-time job? With what social security? One that belongs to a dead guy? Maybe join a dating site while you're at it and see how well that works out, genius. There is no starting over anymore for you. It's over. You ARE nothing. Not only that, but you might be dying. Just look at how badly your rashes have gotten, and then there's that puking episode back at the motel. Even if you did have a chance to start again—the odds of which are laughable—it wouldn't matter because you're probably going to lose your mind and die soon, anyway.

I still have Erin.

And look at how Owen and your own damn wife reacted to you. She'll turn you away just as they did too. Do you really want to ruin that for your last remaining child? Scar her for life? Traumatize her just as you did to

Margie and Owen? It's best if you just leave her alone. Don't get involved. You won't be able to live with yourself if she sees you now.

But—

What part of "You have nothing left to lose" do you not understand? You have no reason to hold yourself back from what you need to do. I ask again: Why were you brought back if you have no other options?

What was this voice? Peter had assumed that it was his subconscious or something, but it didn't seem like that at all. It didn't even feel like his own mind speaking to him. It existed somewhere both inside and yet outside of his mind, like an in-between place.

I was brought back because a man wanted to defy death. He wanted to validate his own ego and conquer God. I exist for no other reason other than that.

There has to be a better reason as to why you were brought back. It's just as the doctor said—your existence precedes your essence. What is your essence?

To avenge Jack.

It made sense. He was a revenant. A specter returned from the grave to inflict vengeance upon those who had wronged him and his loved ones. That was why he was brought back.

If you knew that someone who had hurt your children was out there, unpunished, would you sit and do nothing? Even if Franklin Delahunty isn't off the hook and is awaiting trial, or got off on a light sentence, this is your opportunity to make justice personal. Avenge yourself. Avenge Jack.

Yet to kill? Could he really do that?

Peter thought about how the autopsy report described his son's death. His head had been mashed into pieces. Then he thought about Franklin, going off skateboarding with his friend, unscathed of what he had done.

I won't kill him, Peter concluded. *I'll compromise. I won't kill Franklin because Peter Murphy is not a murderer. However, I won't stand by and let him get away with this. I'll give him a night he'll never forget. I'll make him live with it forever. I'll fuck him up so badly that he'll never walk right again. The legal system be damned—this is* my *justice.*

"I'm gonna do it, Jack," he said. "I'm gonna make him pay."

The red-orange sun mulled at the bottom of the sky. It would be full dark soon. A wind blew by and swayed Peter where he stood, and then he made his way out of the cemetery.

32.

It was almost midnight. The streets were deserted. Peter decided not to park too close to the Delahunty residence. There were plenty of dark spaces between the streetlights, so Peter rolled the truck to a stop in between patches of light and killed the engine.

That awful ache in his head returned, and it quietly throbbed in the front of his head. Peter popped some more aspirin. Since leaving the cemetery, Peter felt feverish. Everything was starting to seriously hurt. Sharp pains cut through his abdomen and chest, and his skin felt as it if were perpetually burning, like his whole body had just gotten tattooed. It was unbearable and uncomfortable.

Yet, the pain and discomfort took a back seat compared to where he was emotionally. He was scared shitless. He knew that he had no reason to be apprehensive, but he was. His knees shook and his hands trembled like an old arthritic's hands. Inside his chest, he felt Angela Fairhardt's heart pumping aggressively.

Part of him just wanted to drive away and go somewhere quiet to await his fate. The other part told him to stop being such a coward. He knew that whatever evidence he would potentially leave behind—blood, hair, skin flakes, whatever—would lead directly to a dead man, so he had that advantage. Even if he was arrested, chances were he was going to die or lose awareness before a trial would even begin.

This needs to be done, he reminded himself. *I can't betray Jack. It's all I have left now. Stay focused.*

Before he got out, he checked his gun. He pulled back on the slide to examine the bullet in the chamber. He remembered his compromise. Murder was not the goal, but he would use the gun to take control of the situation if things got out of hand, or maybe fire off a warning shot. He slipped the gun into the front of his pants, took the duct tape and knife from the glove compartment, and got out.

It was surreal to walk through this neighborhood, knowing what he intended to do. There was an air of triviality to everything. Outwardly, all seemed normal, like he was just taking a late-night stroll. The only sounds were a few crickets and some faraway dog barking. A night like any other, except it wasn't.

Peter turned onto Byron Street. The Delahunty residence came into view. The sprinklers were off, and the watery reflection of pool water danced against the trees in the backyard. He looked up and down the street, then crossed and stepped onto the front yard. There were two cars in the driveway. One was a van, and the other was a smaller, much newer looking car.

Of course, Peter thought. *A new car to replace the totaled one. Cynthia certainly has money to throw around, doesn't she?*

A single light was on in a window on the second floor. Somebody was awake. Peter went around the side of the house and climbed the fence surrounding the backyard. There was a back porch with a sliding glass door, and Peter could see a kitchen through the glass. A lamp glowed on the table, and Cynthia Delahunty came into view. Quickly, Peter scurried into the shadows and observed from afar.

The Modern Prometheus

Cynthia was dressed in a bathrobe and had her hair up in a towel. She strolled through the kitchen with a phone pressed to her ear. Vaguely, Peter could hear her voice, but couldn't make out anything that she was saying. She took a bowl covered with tinfoil from the refrigerator and stepped out of view. The light went out and her voice faded away. Peter slithered out of the shadows and crept past the porch to the other side of the house.

There was an open window with a fan running in it. He stood on his tiptoes and peeked in. The room was lit, but at the angle he was at, he couldn't tell what it was. As far as he could see, Cynthia was nowhere nearby.

Carefully, Peter pushed the window up, took the fan out of the frame and gently placed it against the floor in the room, then climbed through.

He found himself in what looked like a study. A leather chair sat before a big mahogany computer desk with an expensive monitor on it. A lamp next to the monitor was on, and it illuminated several framed photographs on the wall over the desk.

In one photo, a younger Cynthia Delahunty proudly stood behind Franklin, who wore a baseball uniform and looked no older than ten. Franklin was holding a baseball bat in one hand and a big blue ribbon that read "WORLD CHAMP" on it in the other. Another photo featured Franklin standing on a cliff with his arms out, wearing a backpack and shorts, with a view of the White Mountains behind him.

There was more. A glass cabinet stood in a corner of the room, filled with trophies. Peter approached the cabinet and peeked at them. "SECOND PLACE JUNIOR INVENTOR" read one. "HONORABLE MENTION IN ROBOTICS" read another. A very large and tall trophy at the top read, "GRAND PRIZE FOR BEST OF SHOW IN TECHNICAL WONDER".

Among those trophies was yet another framed photo of Franklin as a young elementary school student. He was showing off a remote-controlled race car that he had apparently designed himself. The car sat on a table that had a sign with Franklin's name on it, and Franklin himself was holding a controller and smiling with two missing front teeth. "FIFTH GRADE SCIENCE FAIR 2014 PARTHUM ELEMENTARY" was inscribed in the corner.

So, the little murderer is a whiz kid, Peter thought.

A toilet flushed. Peter nearly grabbed the gun from his pants but refrained. He stood, staring at a door across from him. A light switch was heard clicking, followed by footsteps.

Peter swallowed. He approached the door and kept his hand on the gun. For a moment he stood, listening, but nothing could be heard. With his feminine hand, he grabbed the doorknob, turned it, and opened the door slowly.

Beyond was a dark corridor with what looked like a living room at the end of it. He could see a couch and the glow of a television.

Peter drew the pistol and went down the corridor, mindful of the wooden paneling.

Cynthia crossed the living room, entering Peter's line of sight, and then stepped out of view. Peter froze. After several seconds, she appeared again and sat down on the couch with her back facing him. Peter proceeded.

The living room was large. A fish tank sat next to a large flat-screen TV, and a home bar was set up in the corner. Cynthia sat with her feet on the coffee table, watching some late-night sitcom.

Peter lunged forward, wrapped his arm around the woman's head so that the bend of his arm covered her mouth, and pressed the gun against her temple. "Don't scream."

The woman screamed. Her voice muffled against Peter's arm, and she struggled to get up from the couch. One of her feet knocked over a glass of wine to the floor.

"I said don't scream. I have a gun and I'll shoot you right now if you don't shut up." He jabbed the gun against her temple harder. "Don't speak unless I say, don't move unless I say. I want you to answer my questions with a nod or a head shake. Do you understand?"

The woman nodded.

"Your name is Cynthia Delahunty, right?"

She nodded.

"Is your son Franklin?"

The woman hesitated, and then shook her head.

"You're lying to me. I know he's here. I saw the new car out front, and a light was on in one of the windows on the second floor."

Peter felt teeth digging into his flesh, and he let go of Cynthia's head. She stood and shouted: "Frankie! Frankie, get out of the—"

Peter flew around the couch and swatted the pistol across her face. She fell to the floor, grabbing her cheek. The towel wrapped around her hair came undone, and her hair fluttered about in wet strands. He got on top of her, shoved the gun between her eyes, and clapped his hand over her mouth.

"Don't you dare make another peep or I'll kill you. Don't try it. I'm going to take my hand off your mouth, and you're not to say a word, or I'll kill you. Do you understand?"

Cynthia's eyes watered and a tear ran down the side of her face from the corner of her eye. She nodded.

When Peter took his hand off her mouth, she hoarsely whispered, "I have money."

"I'm not interested in your money. Now flip over on your belly."

"Please—don't!"

"I'm not interested in that, either." Peter gestured with the gun. "On your belly."

Struggling, Cynthia rolled over. Peter grabbed her by the wrists, tucked her hands against her lower back, and began duct taping them together.

"Listen, mister, I don't know what you want. I'll do what you say. Just don't hurt my son."

"Shut up."

"Please, he's all I've got left. I can't—"

Peter whipped the back of her head with the gun. "I said shut up!"

A voice called from upstairs: "Mom?"

Footsteps sounded directly over the living room. Peter wrapped more duct tape around Cynthia's head and mouth, then grabbed her ankles and taped them together as well.

The footsteps came down the stairs and approached the living room. Peter got off Cynthia and flew to a dark corner. Cynthia tried to scream, to warn her son somehow, but her cries were impotent against the tape. She squirmed, jerking her arms and legs, trying to break free. She looked like a struggling worm.

"Mom, did you call me?"

Peter glued himself against the wall. The gun trembled in his grip. *This is it*, he thought.

Franklin appeared in the doorway wearing pajama bottoms and a T-shirt. His eyes were squinting, disturbed by the bright TV. "Mom, what's with all the—"

Peter emerged and swung the pistol against the back of the kid's head. Franklin fell to his hands and knees. Before he was able to react, Peter was already on him, wrapping the duct tape around his face and binding his hands behind his back.

Franklin, now comprehending the situation, got up and shoved himself backward, slamming Peter against the wall. Peter responded by whacking the pistol against Franklin's head a few more times, hard enough for Peter to feel blood splatter against his arm, then threw the kid to the floor and grabbed at his feet. Franklin grunted and moaned and flailed his legs like an animal. One of his feet hit Peter on the nose and knocked his sunglasses off. Peter managed to grab one foot and locked it under his arm, and he began wrapping duct tape around the ankle while Franklin's free foot kicked at his back and head. Once Peter had a few loops done, he leaned down against Franklin's other leg, got the other foot, and began taping them together.

The Delahuntys were under control. Peter stood before them as they struggled, their pleas and cries muffled. It took him a few moments to regain his composure. Breathing was difficult through the bandages. His body shook violently from adrenaline and terror. Franklin looked up at him, and Peter could see him begging with his eyes.

Peter became overcome with doubt. *I can't do this. What am I doing?*

You NEED to do this. Think about what this kid did to your baby. Think about how Jack's head got literally destroyed. And why? Because of HIM. It's too late. Now or never.

Peter pinched the bridge of his nose and exhaled, trying to get a grip on himself. Finally, he sat on the recliner. "I have a couple of things to say to you two."

They didn't listen. They continued to writhe and try to scream.

"Listen to me, goddamn it!" He pointed the gun at them.

They stopped struggling and lay on their sides, staring at him.

"I'm not here for your money or your possessions. I'm here for a very specific reason. I want to make sure that you both understand what that reason is, so I will allow you two to speak. That means I'm going to cut slits in the tape on your mouths, but if you try to scream, I'll kill you. Do you understand?"

They nodded.

Peter rested the gun on the arm of the recliner, drew the pocketknife and carefully cut slits in the tape over Cynthia and Franklin's mouths.

"What do you want from us?" Franklin managed. "Why are you hurting my mom?"

"Don't play dumb with me."

"Mister, listen," Cynthia gasped. "I have a safe upstairs. I can give you the code. I can—"

"I told you that I don't want anything from you. What I want is *him*." He pointed at Franklin. "There are things he needs to be held accountable for."

"Accountable?" Cynthia stammered. "For what?"

"I didn't do anything!" Franklin shouted.

Peter shot him an offended glare, his eyes radiating through the bandages. "Excuse me?"

"I didn't do anything," Franklin said again, this time not as confident.

Peter flew at him and kicked him in the face. Franklin rolled over. Peter got on a knee, grabbed him by the hair and began slamming his face into the floor.

"Stop hurting my boy!" Cynthia cried. "He's done nothing wrong!"

Peter ceased the abuse and pointed at her. "Why wouldn't I hurt him? Tell me! Tell me he's done nothing wrong again! I dare you!"

"He's supposed to go to the University of Boston next year... he's already been accepted. Please, he has dreams. He has so much to live for. He could make hospital equipment and machines. He has a future, mister."

"My son didn't have such a privilege!" Peter stood and began stomping on Cynthia's head. With every impact his foot had with her face, he felt the floorboards shift.

"Leave my mom alone!"

Peter stopped and turned his attention to Franklin. "What you've done is beyond hurt. The consequences of your actions have caused irreparable damage to human life. I can't forgive. A man and his son are dead because of you!" Peter kicked him in the face again. Franklin spat out a wad of blood and a tooth.

The rage was like a hurricane. It drove Peter's every action. Any doubt or guilt he had felt up to this point faded as he thought about the description the autopsy report gave regarding his son. To a degree, Peter even enjoyed listening to Franklin proclaim his innocence. It was so offensive that it only fueled his anger at him, to see this kid blatantly lie about his actions and refuse accountability for them.

"Keep saying it's not your fault." Peter lifted his foot and began stomping on Franklin's face. He felt the kid's nose break, felt his teeth crack, heard him gurgle and choke as blood filled his mouth.

Once the beating stopped, Franklin lay helplessly on his back, his face purple and swelling. Peter took the obituary from his pocket and held it before his face. "This was my child. You robbed me of my child. You're going to tell me you've done nothing wrong?"

Franklin's eyes widened at the obituary. "I didn't... didn't do it."

"You *would* deny it!" Peter shouted.

"The car accident!" Cynthia shouted. "You're talking about the car accident?"

Peter turned to her. "What the fuck else would I be talking about?"

"Please don't kill him," Cynthia said. "It was an accident. He's so young."

"I'm sorry." Franklin cried. "I didn't mean to. It was dark. It wasn't my fault."

"Wasn't your fault?" Peter flew at Franklin like a leopard, grabbing his hair, ready to slam his face into the floor a few more times. "Your actions lead directly to the deaths of myself and my child."

"I don't understand. You?"

"I'm a god damn revenant, you little shit."

"It was the teacher's fault!" Cynthia howled.

Peter let go of Franklin's hair and stood. "What did you just say to me?"

"It's true. It wasn't my son's fault. It was the teacher."

"You have some fucking balls to say that to me."

"No. It's true. I swear to God, it's true."

"That's a lie. You're just saying that to stop me. Your son can't get out of this."

"It's true." Cynthia raised her bloodied face from the floor. The look in her eyes was sincere. "The Highway Department and the state police spent two weeks investigating the crash, examining tire marks and the damage done to both cars. They determined that the teacher cut a lane of traffic as he was merging onto the interstate. The police think he was distracted, maybe by his son. It was dark and raining. The back left of the teacher's car clipped the front of my son's, and it caused both cars to spin out of control."

Peter took a step back. "You're lying."

"It's the truth," Franklin gurgled. "That guy, Peter—he caused the accident. He hit me. He killed himself and his son."

"No."

"Yes, it's true," Cynthia said. "I have the proof. My son was arrested, but the case against him was thrown out. I still have the court documents. They're upstairs. Read them. Read them, god damn it! It's all true. My son is innocent!"

Peter didn't move. He stood so still in the dark that he could have been mistaken for a scarecrow. His mind scrambled to fight the cognitive dissonance that he was experiencing. His legs went numb, and to keep from falling, his hand snaked out and grabbed the arm of the couch.

Cynthia went on, "I'm sorry for what happened to your friends or family, sir. But that is the truth. The police confirmed it, and whatever legal proceedings Frankie had to go through, he already did. He's been through hell." She turned to look at her disfigured son. "Frankie? Talk to me, please tell me you're still alive. Say something."

"Mom," Franklin moaned. "Mom...I can't see. It hurts so much."

Peter slunk away, grabbing the sides of his head. "No," he whispered. *No, not like this.*

"Please," Franklin begged. "Let me and my mom go. We're sorry. I'm sorry. I live with this every day."

"My son still has a chance to live. Just... please let us go."

Their voices faded. All senses numbed. Peter became utterly consumed by everything that he had just heard. He felt like he was going to vomit. He bent over, clutching his chest and abdomen, and began gagging. He screamed. It was a heinous sound, filled with anguished moans and high pitches of grief. Franklin and Cynthia stared at their attacker as he screamed. The sounds he made mortified them.

Then Peter saw the mirror. It was a small one hanging over the home bar. Peter saw himself, and he resembled some bandaged Quasimodo in the dark with his shoulders slouched and his eyes wide open. Even through the bandages, he could see The Expression.

Raw emotion took over. Filled with abhorrence and denial, he smashed the mirror with his fist, and shards of it rained on the bar, rattling the glasses on it.

"What are you doing?" Cynthia said.

Peter turned around. "You lie. No, I won't accept this."

"We're not... lying." Franklin croaked.

"You lie! You killed my child! *YOU KILLED MY JACK!*"

Peter grabbed the gun off the arm of the recliner and shot Franklin in the face. The kid's body seized violently, and then he went still.

Cynthia screamed her son's name. Peter shot her in the forehead, and she went still as well.

The stench of gun smoke lingered in the air. For a moment, time seemed to stop, and Peter stared at the two bodies on the floor in front of him. He was astonished by the destructive power that he never knew he possessed. Blood poured from the heads of Franklin and Cynthia Delahunty and sank into the carpet, looking almost black in the dark.

Once the astonishment passed, the gravity of what he had just done hit him. The Delahuntys did not move. Peter stepped back in bewilderment.

What did I just do? How did I do this?

No, I didn't just do this—I couldn't, I couldn't have done this!

A loud ringing sounded in his ears, and the room suddenly felt like it was getting bigger. All sensations in his body became enunciated, and he felt like he was floating. His mind slowly disassociated for several moments, and then reality returned in full clarity.

Terror took charge. He fled the living room and entered the anteroom. He wasn't thinking clearly. All he knew was that he needed to get away from this—from this horrible thing that he had just done. Panicking, he grabbed the knob of the front door and found it locked. He unlocked it, yanked the door open, and ran out.

Peter sprinted down Byron Street, and then turned onto the road where the truck was parked. He could see the shape of it in between the streetlights, and he got inside and started it. The tires screamed against the pavement. When they finally gripped,

The Modern Prometheus

the truck flew down the street. Peter's body jerked from side to side as he sped through the neighborhood, taking sharp turns all the way back to I-495.

Unbeknownst to Peter, a neighbor of the Delahuntys had heard the screams and gunshots, and he stepped outside just in time to see Peter fleeing the house.

Jayson Robert Ducharme

IV.
DEATH

33.

It was a cool morning. It seemed like for months the heat would not abate, but today the temperature was only seventy degrees, and the sky was cloudy, so Helena took the opportunity to get some yard work done.

After having eggs and coffee, she put on her work jeans, which were stained on the knees from wearing them anytime she had to do work outside, and pulled on a pair of gardening gloves. She prepared quietly, not wanting to disturb her daughter, who was snoozing on the couch. Margie slumbered quietly with her wool blanket pulled up to her chin, her face exhausted and pale. For a moment, Helena took a moment to pity her daughter.

Margie had been rattled since arriving at the house a few nights ago, and she kept to herself, mostly watching TV. Helena wished her daughter could be shown some mercy. Quietly, she opened the back door and stepped outside.

The rain gutters needed to be cleared. They were still full of leaves from the previous autumn. In her more youthful years, Helena would have done it as soon as the snow cleared, but now that she was older, any task that demanded prolonged endurance was taxing on her aging body, so she had put it off. This morning, though, she felt up for it.

There was a small wooden shed behind the house that had all the yard supplies. She unlocked the padlock that kept the two rickety doors closed, opened one, and stepped inside the musky, humid shed. It stench of dead grass and wood lingered in the air. An assortment of tools hung on the wall over the work bench, and a green riding mower sat near the back. Carefully, Helena navigated around the mower and found her six-foot-long ladder. With some strain, she managed to pick it up and drag it outside.

Carefully, she set the ladder against the back of the house and began to ascend it. She passed one of the windows that peered into Erin's room. The young girl was sitting at the desk by the window, scribbling in a notebook. Helena quickly went up to the top of the ladder so that she wouldn't get caught snooping, and began examining the gutter, which was filled to the brim with mossy leaves. It had rained recently, and the leaves were still wet.

With every handful of gunky leaves she took up and pitched to the ground below, her thoughts turned to her son-in-law,

Peter. It was difficult to not think about him. She had grieved Jack inconsolably, but with Peter it was different. With Peter, she felt guilty. She knew that she had not treated him the way that he had deserved. Ever since her own marriage crumbled, she swore to ensure that Margie would never experience the same thing she had with a man. Reggie had been such an awful husband and father, and the way the marriage had ended was the worst of it all. It brought Helena immeasurable shame. She had chased off a lot of men from her daughter over the years, but she never managed to scare away Peter.

Maybe that was why she had wound up liking him as much as she did. In the beginning, she had disliked him immensely. Disliked his high cheek bones and his bright Irish eyes and how timid he was. She had intimidated him, doubted him, and even threatened him, but in the end, Peter always remained loyal to her daughter. And despite her behavior toward him, he visited her for the holidays, sent her cards, offered to come up and help around the house, and even called for her birthday.

When she had witnessed the birth of her first grandchild, and she saw the way Peter held Erin and cherished her with Margie, that resentment and mistrust began to relax. Peter wasn't Reggie. Reggie hadn't even been present for Margie's own birth. He had been drinking with his buddies downtown and didn't even show up to the hospital until the next day. In the years since then, she had watched Peter provide and secure for his family, getting them a house and plenty of food in their bellies. Shortly before his death, he had even been talking about taking everyone to Disney World in Florida.

Peter had been a good, capable man. The greatest regret that Helena carried with her in this whole situation was that she had never apologized for how she had treated him. Now she never could.

Just as she picked up another glob of moldy leaves and tossed them, her pocket vibrated. Frustrated, Helena tucked one of her gloves under her arm and dug her phone out. It was Peter's brother, Owen.

Helena didn't know Owen very well and only met him during family occasions. It was even rarer that he ever called. They had each other's numbers mostly out of formality. She spoke to him briefly after she had brought Margie home from the hospital, but before that was during the funeral in January. Through word of mouth, she knew that he had been drowning himself in booze since Peter and Jack died.

She answered, "Hello? Owen?"

"Uh, hi," Owen said. "How are you, Helena?"

"I'm all right. How are you, Owen? I don't hear from you very often."

"I'm… okay." He paused. "Do you know where Margie is?"

The Modern Prometheus

Helena took a few steps down the ladder and peered into the living room window. Margie was just waking, sitting up on the couch and rubbing her face.

"She's with me, up in Manchester," Helena said. "Why do you ask?"

"I tried calling her phone a couple of times." Owen cleared his throat. "She hasn't answered."

Helena suddenly realized that not once had she noticed her daughter using her phone since she arrived. "I haven't seen her using it. I think she may have left it back at the house in Atkinson."

"Is everything all right?"

It was a loaded question. Helena considered her next few words. "It's been rough. She's staying with me and Erin for a bit. You're aware that Erin has been with me while Margie has been at the house going to therapy and whatnot?"

"Yeah, she told me that. Do you know why she left? And even left her phone there?"

"No, I think she just needed to get out of that house for a bit."

"Was it because she saw something?"

Helena's heart skipped a beat. She remembered what Margie had said—about what she saw back at the house that had prompted her to come to Manchester. She decided to lie. "I don't know if she saw anything. Why?"

"I just thought I saw something recently. Something weird. But I had been drinking. Heavily. I can't stop thinking about it."

"What did you see?"

Owen took a long time to reply. "You know, forget about it. Forget I said anything. Sorry to bother you."

He hung up. Helena stared at her phone. Again, she peeked through the window at her daughter on the couch.

Margie says she saw Peter. Owen says he saw 'something' and inquired if Margie left the house because she saw it too. What if...

Helena dismissed the thought. She stuffed her phone back in her pocket and slipped her glove back on. *Rubbish. It's absurd. Can't believe I even thought of it.*

She climbed up to the gutters and got back to work. She decided to not tell Margie about the phone call. The last thing her daughter needed was to be disturbed by such an idea.

34.

The lake glimmered beneath the morning sun. No life disturbed this quiet besides a family of loons floating on the water far out in the distance. One of them called out, its squawk echoing in the solitude.

The lake was somewhere deep in the woods east of the town of Pelham, about a twenty-five-minute drive from Methuen. After what happened with the Delahuntys, Peter fled until he got too paranoid to drive on the highway, then pulled off and decided to try and hide. All night, he sat with his back against a tree, staring at the lake as the sun slowly crept into view.

Nowhere felt safe anymore. Not the house back in Atkinson, nor that crummy motel in Salem. Never had Peter ever felt this way. There were a lot of things that he had never felt since waking up in this new life, but what he felt now was worse than anything else. More than ever, he was alone without any idea of what to do.

Peter kept hearing Franklin crying as he mangled his face with his foot, and kept seeing how his body had jerked violently as if struck by lightning when he shot him. He kept hearing Cynthia's horrified shrieks, shouting her child's name just before he shot her too.

Mostly, he thought about what Cynthia had told him about the accident. He mulled over this information, and it only made him disassociate further.

I'm a murderer, he kept thinking. *I murdered a young boy and his mother. I didn't just murder them, but I tortured them as well.*

All the pain and grief that he had experienced since awakening in Jacob Abbott's cabin had been accumulating and compartmentalizing within him the longer he stayed alive. All of it boiled together over the course of a few short days, and was aimed at and unleashed on Franklin Delahunty and his mother. Now there was a strong possibility that they both were entirely innocent in this whole affair and that Peter was the only one to blame. And yet he had tortured and murdered them.

Why had he shot them? He had never intended to kill them. The only reason why he had the gun was to use it as potential deterrence or for control. Yet, when Cynthia had told him that he was responsible for killing himself and his child, he just lost control. He had lost control over his mind, his emotions, and his body. It was like he needed to destroy this frightening reality that was materializing before him, and by instinct he had grabbed the gun and destroyed—

—*the truth?*

Still, his mind tried to rationalize: *That boy murdered you and your son.*

I put that boy in circumstances where he accidentally caused the deaths of me and my son. It wasn't his fault. It was my fault.

How do you know that's true? What if Cynthia was lying?

If Cynthia was lying, then why was Franklin not in prison? Why was he going off to college? Cynthia insisted that he still had a future.

The Modern Prometheus

It was like a war going off inside his head, with both sides of his conscience lashing out at one another; one side that knew the truth, and the other that didn't want to believe it.

Many times, Peter considered his gun. He had taken it out of his pants and rested it in the dirt at his feet. He wondered if he should return from whence he came—to finish the job that he was about to initiate while kneeing on his son's grave. Had he done it then and there, the Delahuntys would still be alive. What was stopping him now, especially since he knew that Jacob couldn't bring Jack back? Now that he knew his time was running out? Now that he was a murderer?

Peter tried to lick his lips, but his bandages made it difficult. The gauze was starting to get heavy and bloated. He pressed his hands against his face and felt how moist the bandages were becoming, absorbing all the fluids that were leaking out of him.

He licked Timothy Saunders' teeth. One of those teeth felt loose, and Peter tongued at it. Without any effort at all, the tooth pushed out of his gum and slipped into his bottom lip.

Dispirited, Peter undid the bandages around his mouth and spat the tooth out in a wad of blood. He began running his fingers along his top front teeth, and he felt the left canine wiggle. He gripped it between his thumb and forefinger, twisted it, and the tooth popped out. Blood pooled into his mouth again and he spat out another red glob into the grass. He held the tooth before his eyes for a few moments, then flicked it away and covered his mouth with the bandages again.

I'm falling apart, he thought. *Just let me die. I'm a mistake of nature. Why couldn't I have just stayed dead and been spared all this?*

Every second he remained in this nightmare, the worse it became.

I wish I stayed with you, Jack, he thought.

Suddenly, something felt funny inside his head. For a long time, he sat there, stricken with a sensation that he had never felt before. He felt dizzy, and almost fell over, but nudged his arm out and stopped himself on his elbow.

His thoughts suddenly became a jumbled mess, crisscrossing inside his head. One train of thought began, then was suddenly severed, cut off by another train of thought. Pressure accumulated in his head. It was like his brain was trying to break out the front of his skull. Desperately, he clawed out the bottle of aspirin from his pocket, but when he unscrewed the cap, he found that it was empty. He let out an agitated cry and pitched the empty bottle away.

My head—something's wrong with my mind. GOOD GOD WHAT IS HAPPENING TO MY MIND?

The pain became so pronounced that it felt like the inside of his skull was on fire. Then his nose got clogged, and he felt warm gushing in the bandages above his lips. Quickly, he undid

The Modern Prometheus

the bandages over his mouth and nose, and blood poured from his nostrils.

"Jesus Christ!"

The blood kept pouring, stinking of iron, turning black in the dirt. That was when the convulsions began. It started with tremors in his hands, and then his arms and legs began spasming. It became hard to breathe.

I'm suffocating I'm suffocating I'm suffocating I'm—

And then all thought went away. Peter's eyes rolled into the back of his head, and he fell over into the bloody dirt, convulsing. After what felt like an eternity, he went still.

35.

An hour later, he slowly regained consciousness. Instantly, he knew something significant had happened to him, but he couldn't explain it what it was to himself. It felt like his skull was empty, like his brain had just leaked out of his face. That was silly, of course, because he was still thinking and alive, but it sure as hell felt that way.

He became confused. Why was he in this forest? How did he get here? *Why was there blood everywhere?*

"Oh God." Peter sat up and crawled away from the blood. "What happened to me? Somebody help me!"

The memories of what he had done came to him violently, but he couldn't understand where they came from or what the context was. It horrified him. He saw a bruised and bloodied teenage boy, and he saw himself bringing his foot down on the face of a terrified woman. He heard gunshots and smelled the smoke, and in his mind's eye, he saw these two people die, and himself holding the gun that did it.

I killed two people, but… I don't—I don't remember why!

WHY DID I DO THIS?

As he sat there hyperventilating, he closed his eyes and focused, trying to walk himself through what he did remember leading up to these memories of murder. The car accident, the autopsy report, the woman (*Cindy? Claudia? Was her name Claudia?*) telling him that he caused the car accident that killed his son.

My son? Jack. JACK.

Slowly, the fog in his mind cleared, and he could remember most everything. The only things he struggled with were the mother's name, where she and her son (*Franklin, I know his name was Franklin*) had lived, and how he had gotten in the house. There were pockets in his memory where information should have been, and no matter how hard Peter tried, he couldn't remember.

I'm losing mental clarity. I'm losing myself.

The Modern Prometheus

It was all so much. He began to weep. "I'm a monster," he croaked.

Peter Murphy isn't a monster, a familiar voice interjected. It was the very same voice in his mind that had spoken to him back at the cemetery.

Yes, I am.

Peter Murphy is dead.

No… No, I'm still here.

Peter Murphy isn't a monster because Peter Murphy is dead. Peter died in a car accident six months ago.

But I am *Peter Murphy. I possess his mind and his emotions.*

Are they really his emotions? Are they really his thoughts? Would Peter Murphy ever consider torturing and murdering people? Are those really the thoughts, feelings, and intentions of Peter Murphy? Or are they of someone else?

Who else would I be?

You possess Angela Fairhardt's and Timothy Saunders' organs, bones and limbs. Does that mean you're Angela and Timothy, too?

No? Yes? I don't know.

They're dead too. So, you can't be them, either. You're not Peter, Angela or Tim at all.

Peter stood up. His senses became amplified. The glittering waves of the lake ahead suddenly hurt his eyes, and the calls of the loons out there became somehow deafening. It was like he was experiencing manic euphoria.

There is nothing in you that resembles Peter Murphy anymore. Peter's wife and brother refuse to acknowledge his existence, his co-workers and friends don't recognize you and consider him dead. There is so much of your body that has been replaced or removed, so can you even really call it Peter Murphy's body anymore? Your personality, your actions, your behavior, not even your body—none of that is Peter Murphy, is it?

But who else could I possibly be?

What is death? It is the cessation of existence, is it not? Once you're dead, the only things left of you are your worldly possessions and the psychological recollections people have of you. All abstractions or material extensions of the deceased, but not the deceased themselves. Peter Murphy has ceased to exist. Parts of your body are his, but it is no different from an organ or limb transplant. Just because you get a heart transplant from a dead donor doesn't mean that donor is alive. You merely possess parts of Peter's dead body, but that doesn't mean you're him.

I still have his memories.

Memories are all that's left of who he was. Even then, you're beginning to struggle with recalling those memories, aren't you? And what of Timothy Saunders and Angela Fairhardt? Peter, Timothy and Angela all make up your body, but you yourself are none of them because they're all dead.

So, what am I?

The Modern Prometheus

Something that should not exist, and yet you do. Is it really right to say that you shouldn't exist? If that were the case, you wouldn't exist at all.

Peter grabbed the sides of his head and squeezed. "No, I'm losing myself," he grunted. "I can't deal with this."

You have to, that voice pressed. *Are you even human? What exactly is the definition of "human"?*

It means… relating to or possessing characteristics of human beings. I can stand upright, I have cognitive functions capable of abstract thought, and can express articulate speech. I possess all the characteristics of something that is human, and yet…?

You're not natural. What does "natural" even mean?

It means existing or caused by nature. Not made or caused by humankind.

Precisely. You are human, but you are not a natural *human. You were not conceived and born of nature. You were conceived through science, and Peter, Tim and Angela were all combined into one body to create you. As such, you are something completely new. Something not quite human, but something else. Something that possesses all the characteristics of a human but is in itself unnatural and different from a human.*

But what is happening to my body? What is happening to my mind? Why am I falling apart like this? Why does it feel like I can't control how I think or remember things anymore?

It's because your body and mind are rejecting Peter. They are rejecting Angela and Timothy too. It is part of your evolution, taking on a new form and consciousness as an unnatural being.

What does this mean?

Death is merely a transition from one form of existence to another. You can, in fact, create life out of death. Human beings are capable of that now, and you are evidence of this. Human beings can evolve from a natural state to an unnatural state. It means you can become something more than human.

Can I?

Peter, Angela and Timothy have all ceased living as their natural beings and evolved into a single unnatural being. Honor their sacrifice to create you.

Peter's hands tightened into fists. He looked down at the gun in the grass, and he reached down and took it up. He was finally seeing the glory in all of this. The fact that he was standing here, breathing, thinking, and feeling, was an act of rebellion against the constraints of nature—against God itself. Why stop there? How could he have even considered throwing it all away?

The world was not ready for him, but that was okay. He was above life and death, because he knew that he possessed power over both. He would carve out his own little piece of the world, and he would utilize this newfound power to change humanity. Only now he realized the gift that Jacob Abbott had given him.

He knew exactly where to start.

36.

Marjorie Murphy stared into the light-brown coffee within her mug, watching the creamer she had added swirl around. One moment, she was pouring the creamer and getting ready for the day, and the next she was somewhere else, far away in her mind.

"Honey?"

Margie blinked. Her mother stepped into the kitchen through the back door. She was sweating and wearing her yard work clothes and gloves. Margie cleared her throat and returned the creamer to the fridge. "Hi," she said with some embarrassment.

"Doing all right?" Helena pulled off her gloves and set them on the table. "It seems like you've been doing a little better since yesterday."

It was true that she had been practically catatonic the first few nights after she arrived at the house, but in her opinion, she had every reason to be. "I guess."

"They're reopening the museum on Parkland this Tuesday. It might do you some good to get out for a bit. You know, with

Erin. It's been a long time since you two did anything together. It might be helpful for both of you."

It was obvious what she was trying to do. Maybe she was right to some degree. Margie knew that she had been an awful and self-absorbed person, and her thoughts turned to Erin.

"Yeah," Margie said. She stood in the doorway of the kitchen and looked across the living room at the guest bedroom door, which had been shut all day.

Every time she thought of her daughter—her only child now—she felt horrible and guilty. She couldn't stop thinking about how she had behaved toward her daughter these past several months.

"I'm going to take a shower," Helena called as she went down the hall. "I'll be back in a bit."

"Sure thing," Margie said. She waited until she heard the shower water start running, then she crossed the living room and knocked on the guest bedroom door. "Erin?"

"Yeah?"

She opened the door. Erin was sitting at the desk by the window, her chin resting on her palm, watching the cars outside zip up and down the street.

For a few moments, Margie was uncertain of what to do. Then she stepped in and knelt next to her daughter. "Do you want to go to a museum on Tuesday?"

Erin didn't take her eyes away from the window. "Not really."

"What about that park near Elm Street? You used to love going over there whenever we came to visit Grandma."

Erin shrugged.

Margie adjusted herself on her knees and leaned forward. "Can you look at me, Erin?"

Erin looked at her. Intense pain was hidden behind that still, cold face

"Listen Erin, I know that I haven't been here for you. And I want to apologize for that. Ever since what happened to your brother and father—it's all been so much to process. I know I neglected you. I should have been stronger for you because you needed me. I'm sorry. I want to do something for you."

"When did you get out of the hospital?" Erin asked plainly.

"I got out the day before I came here. I wanted to make the house look nice, make you a cake, and then surprise you by coming up and taking you home."

"Then why aren't we home?"

Margie's heart skipped a beat. "Something happened."

Erin swallowed and turned her attention back to the window.

"Please." Margie put her hand on Erin's knuckles. "Let me help you. Let's try to go somewhere and do something, as mother and daughter. I want to be close to you again."

Erin's voice cracked. "I just want my life back."

A lump formed in Margie's throat. She wanted the same thing. "I want our lives back too. I want it back every day."

Erin pulled her hand away from her mother's and turned from the window to face her. "You came here crying. You said you saw Dad again."

She heard everything that night, Margie thought morosely. Now she had no idea what to say, because in truth she wasn't really sure what had happened that day back at the house. In fact, it was something she had avoided thinking about.

"Did you really see him?" Erin asked. Now her voice sounded as if it were uncertain and hopeful. "You saw Dad and you got scared?"

"Erin, I didn't see your father."

Scorn crossed her daughter's face. "Why did you come back here saying you did?"

"I don't know what I saw. I haven't… been healthy, honey. And I've been on a lot of medicine. I think I only saw your dad because I wanted to."

"Leave me alone."

The words *"I'm sorry"* nearly passed Margie's lips, but she held back. It felt as if it would be insulting to say them. Silently, Margie stood and stepped out of the room.

God, I'm such a horrible person, Margie thought, sitting down on the couch. Erin probably felt like she had been abandoned by her own mother, and to a degree Margie felt like she couldn't blame her if she did feel that way. She had suffered a complete nervous breakdown after the funeral, and barely functioned as a human, never mind as a mother.

Truth be told, she hadn't initially wanted to tell Erin the truth about going to a mental hospital. She hadn't wanted to fill her daughter's head with images of her mother being put in a straitjacket and locked up in some padded cell. Yet, she also felt that it was her duty as a mother to tell her daughter the truth. The last thing Margie wanted to do was break her daughter's trust—especially now that she was the only child she had left.

Margie's time at Hampstead Hospital had been productive for the most part. She had been nervous about going, since she herself had imagined being put in a straitjacket and locked away in a padded room, but the experience thankfully wasn't quite like that. She had been given a lot of medications and therapy, and even made a friend with a woman who suffered from bipolar disorder in the ward, so she hadn't been completely alone. It wasn't a pleasant experience, but it hadn't been torture, either.

She did wind up staying there longer than she had intended—initially she thought she would be there for a few weeks tops, but ended up staying for three months.

Margie left Hampstead on June 18. Helena had been the one to pick her up, and she had given Margie the tightest hug that she had even gotten since she was a child.

"It's such a relief to see my baby again!" Helena had declared.

On the way home, Margie told Helena that she wanted a day or two to dust and clean the house, talk things over at work, and do a few other things.

"I want the house to look presentable for Erin to come home to," she said. "And I need to make sure everything is good for me to go back to work. Maybe I'll bake a cake for Erin, too."

She explained that she wanted to surprise Erin by driving up on Wednesday, and that she fully intended on getting both their lives back on track. Margie was feeling as well as she could have felt, given the circumstances, and all she wanted to do was see Erin again. Helena dropped her off at the house in Atkinson and told her to call before she came up. Margie told her that she would.

And then, the very next day, *that* happened. Whatever *that* was.

That had truly disturbed Margie's soul. She wasn't even sure now what she had seen. There she had been in the bathroom, washing her face, and then—a ghost? She had heard someone running around the house shouting, and when she investigated, she had seen Peter, or something like him. He had looked gray and purple, and there was something off about his appearance that she couldn't quite place. He had spoken to her. He had *touched* her. Even now, thinking about it, her entire body erupted into gooseflesh.

Margie put the memory away and pressed her hands against her face. A hallucination. That was the only explanation. In her mania and depression, combined with months of different kinds of medications, she had a mirage of her husband coming to visit her. Peter was dead and buried over in Atkinson Cemetery along with her youngest child. He wasn't a ghost or some voodoo zombie. He was gone and she had wanted him back so badly that she had imagined the whole scenario. There was no other explanation. It had felt so real.

Even now, thinking about returning to the house in Atkinson terrified her. Consciously, she knew that her dead husband couldn't possibly be there, but on some instinctive level she was convinced that he was.

How could it have all gone so awry? It seemed Peter and Jack were the only things she could think about anymore. It felt pathetic, but it was true. Maybe she was being too hard on herself. Maybe how she was feeling was the only sane way to feel for a mother and a wife.

Growing up, she had never dreamed of having a family. *A family? Me?* It seemed so foreign. Yet, Margie never had any regrets about marrying Peter or having his children. It was probably her mother's influence that made her grow up thinking that way. Life after Dad went to prison was hard, and her mother had always been embittered by the experience. As such, Margie believed that she was just going to focus on a career, maybe get involved in civil engineering. She knew that she was good at math and science and excelled in those subjects throughout elementary, middle and high school. Dad had been an engineer too, and despite the connotations, Mom was never opposed to the idea because she always said it was good money for a young woman.

Yet, in the back of her mind, Margie always wondered if maybe her mother was giving her the wrong idea about love. While Margie had casually dated since high school, it wasn't until she met Peter did she actually seriously consider marriage. She never intended on abandoning her engineering prospects, but she found herself opening up to the possibility of children for the first time in her life.

Erin was her only remaining child, the last person she had of the family that she had devoted her life to. All at once, she realized just how stupid she had been. Peter and Jack were gone, and they were never coming back, but for the love of God, she still had one child in this world. She should be cherishing that.

"I'm so sorry, Erin," she whimpered.

Slippers scurried across the hardwood floor. Helena came down the hall wearing a bathrobe, freshly cleaned. She saw her daughter in distress and sat down next to her. "Margie? What is it?"

Margie allowed her mother to console her. "I'm a mess."

"It's okay. You need time."

"What I need is to get my damn act together. I've been such a wreck that I'm making myself see dead people."

"Margie—"

"No." She looked at her mother seriously, her grief tamed. "I need to be a mother again. Erin needs me. I've neglected her for too long. Wallowing in my misery hasn't helped her when she needed a mother most."

"Are you sure you don't need more time?"

"There will never be enough time in the world to get over what happened to my baby and husband, Mom. But I still have one child left. And I need to be her mother if I have any hope of surviving this."

"You shouldn't push yourself."

"I have spent the past half year not pushing myself. And where has it gotten me? It's ruined my relationship with my daughter, and now I'm seeing dead people. No, I *will* be the mother Erin needs."

Helena bit her lip, considering all this. "Always remember that I will support you no matter what."

"Thank you. For having faith in me."

Helena kissed her daughter's forehead. "What are you going to do?"

"Whatever Erin needs, I'll give it to her. I owe her so much. But first, I need to eat."

"You left your coffee on the counter. It must be cold by now."

"Ah shoot. You're right. I'll just microwave it. I'm going to eat something and go for a jog."

Helena smiled. "You haven't gone jogging in a long time."

"Not since December." Margie stood, went into the kitchen, took her mug of coffee from the counter, and put it in the microwave.

Helena grabbed the TV remote from the coffee table. Just as she was about to turn the TV on, she spotted the guest room door open a crack. She saw her granddaughter's face peeking out, and the moment they locked eyes, the door shut firmly.

The Modern Prometheus

Once she had some food in her, Margie put on a pair of sweatpants, a sports bra and T-shirt, and then began jogging through the neighborhood towards Elm Street. Her body felt as if it were awakening after a prolonged coma. Weak muscles and hibernating organs started to chug, stretch, and breathe. It may have only been six months, but it wasn't until Margie started running did she realize just how much of a toll grief had taken on her body.

It had been a long run, probably an hour and a half. She went up Elm Street, then through Veteran's Memorial Park. Couples had picnics in the grass and a lone musician tooted his trumpet while sitting on the edge of a concrete fountain. People bustled in and out of coffee shops and walked their dogs up and down the sidewalks. The city was alive. She was alive. The endurance stirred her body and sweat poured down her face and chest. Half a year of misery excreted from her pores.

I'm alive, she kept thinking.

At the end of her run, she turned onto Chestnut Street and made her way back to the neighborhood. By the time she reached Piscataquog Street, she was thoroughly exhausted. Her muscles and bones ached, but she didn't care. She needed this.

Helena's little house came into view. She could see Erin sitting on the curb out front, pitching little pebbles into the street and watching them bounce away.

Margie stopped next to her and hunched down with her hands on her knees, taking heavy breaths. "Hey sweetie, what are you out here for?"

Erin fiddled with her hands nervously. "I don't know."

"Come on. Talk to me."

Erin opened her mouth, stopped herself, and then said, "I'm never going to be okay ever again. But I wanna do the best I can."

"What do you mean?"

Erin got up and hugged her mother. "I'm sorry."

"Oh hun." Margie hugged her child back. "You don't have to be sorry for anything."

"I wanna try."

"Try what?"

"Being happy with just you."

"I want to try and be happy with just you too. You're all I have left now."

"I didn't mean to hate you."

"Shhh. Stop apologizing."

"I can't help it. I'm just so mad and confused. But I don't ever wanna be mad at you again because I don't wanna lose you too."

Margie put her hands on her daughter's shoulders and looked into her eyes. "Erin, I'm going to give you all that I possibly have to give. We will survive this together."

Margie kissed her daughter on the nose, and the two pressed their foreheads together. This was the first time they had shared any kind of affection with each other since Jack and Peter died.

It was also their last intimate moment together.

37.

The afternoon heat was sweltering. The humidity was so thick that it felt like you could cut it with a knife. If there was anything to be thankful for despite this, it was the isolation. There was nothing else around but nature. The silence gave Jacob time to meditate as he worked. The more he thought, the more it propelled him to keep shoveling.

There was no safe place to dump the remains of the decomposing subjects, he had concluded. He was paranoid about disposing them in rivers or lakes, even if he weighed them down. Somehow it felt safer to just bury them in a deep grave. In a way it would be like giving the people he'd treated as tools a proper burial.

After scouting the area, Jacob had found a spot in the woodlands that seemed like a safe space to dispose the bodies about half a mile away from the cabin. All morning, Jacob dug into the ground with an old rusty shovel, wearing nothing but his dress shoes and slacks. Sweat poured down his chest and face as he worked. His entire body felt like it was on fire. This was the most physical labor he'd done in years. It almost felt like penitence.

After about two hours he had managed to create a decent sized hole, about six feet deep and six feet wide. He stuck the shovel into the bottom of the pit and climbed out, sitting at the edge of the hole, wiping perspiration from his eyes. Everything hurt, but he needed to keep going. Once the subjects (*bodies*, he reminded himself, *bodies of people*) were buried, he planned on burning all his research and tools. Once that was finished, he would scrub down the entire cabin from top to bottom.

Just a little deeper, he thought, *and then I'll begin the burial.*

Jacob took a moment to reflect on the early days of the project that led to Peter's creation. He had just gotten his doctorate and was living in a comfortable apartment in Washington, D.C. The next step for his career was to train in a residency program and become licensed to practice in a specific field of medicine. He had secured the funds to pursue this, but he decided to not to take his medical career any further. Instead, he took the money to begin work on creating life.

The Modern Prometheus

The apartment in Washington was no squalid den. It was a spacious place with large, tall rooms, full amenities for the bathroom and kitchen, and skylights in the ceiling of the living room. The only thing that really mattered to Jacob at the time was that he had plenty of living space. Once he moved in with only a suitcase of clothes and several briefcases of his research, he began to slowly fill that apartment to the brim with equipment.

Pipettes, capsule filters, autoclaves, microscopes, scales, mixers, shakers, evaporators, freeze dryers, dry block heaters, mantles, baths, cryostats, reactors, incubators, fume hoods, electro-hydraulic mounting presses, UV irradiation cabinets—anything that he needed at any particular time, he bought and set up in the apartment. After nonstop experimentation, research, trial and error, frustration and lots of tears, he crammed every corner of the apartment with all sorts of gizmos. If one were to walk in—of which nobody except Jacob did, and he made sure of that—they would have to scoot and tip-toe with their arms up to keep from bumping into anything.

After fourteen long, cruel months in that apartment, Jacob had made his first great breakthrough. One night in early October, he had found a large mouse that had gotten snagged in a trap he had set up in his kitchen. Its neck had been snapped in the steel hammer of the trap, and from what Jacob could tell, it had died recently. Carefully, he removed the dead mouse from the trap and brought it to his living room, where most of his chemicals and equipment were.

The moon beamed down through the skylights against his worktable, and he set the mouse on it and began hooking it up with cables and pincers that were wired to a device with several dials on it. He injected the mouse with the necessary fluids, and then turned the dials. After about two minutes, the mouse twitched, and its eyes opened. Jacob took a pen and moved it slowly in vertical motions and observed the mouse's eyes as they followed the tip of the pen. After about thirty seconds of apparent cognitive function, the little mouse had cried out in pain, and then died.

Jacob had set the pen down and placed his hands on the table on either side of the mouse. The poor animal had not stayed alive, but he had successfully reanimated it temporarily. It wasn't much, but it gave him the morale boost he really needed to keep going. It would be quite a leap to move from mouse to man, but Jacob decided to make it happen. He expected to fail many times and knew that he would deplete the rest of his money doing it, but it was attainable.

After that, he sold much of his equipment but held on to anything that he knew was necessary to expand upon what he had already accomplished, and then left Washington. The first big step was to figure out where he could have access to bodies and a private place to work. He stayed in Providence for a time, then Boston, where he met Benjamin O'Toole, who worked at a funeral home in New Hampshire. Benjamin offered to help at the right price, and Jacob had found a secluded cabin in the same state to rent out. His venture took off from there.

Jacob lay down in the grass with his legs dangling in the hole, and he stared up at the sky, thinking. He had made up his mind to kill Peter. He should have done it when he had the chance, and he had almost done it the night Peter escaped. It had been two days now since he last saw him, and Jacob was becoming increasingly paranoid that Peter may never try to contact him. Even though he was already dying, there was no telling what Peter was capable of while he was still fully functional, but part of Jacob still hoped that he could reason with him—to lure him into his final death, so to speak.

Before he could work any further, he needed water. He was dying of thirst and had gone through an entire jug of water since he stepped outside. Jacob got up and walked back.

When the cabin finally came into view, Jacob could hear the vague noise of the phone ringing inside.

Oh no, he thought. He picked up the pace and went through the back door. By the time he entered the living room, the phone had ceased ringing.

God damn it! Shit! How many times has he called?

After several seconds, the phone rang again. Jacob snatched the receiver from the cradle. "Hello?"

"I called four times, Jacob," Peter said, his voice weathered. "Where were you?"

"I'm sorry. I was"—he struggled for an excuse—"I was downstairs, caught up—"

"You know what? It doesn't matter. You answered, so now we can talk."

"What do you want to talk about, Peter?"

"Take a seat. I've been doing a lot of thinking, and I've figured everything out."

Jacob sat on the couch. "I'm listening."

Peter coughed—a sickly sound with audible phlegm. "I've killed them."

Jacob's mouth dried. "What? Who?"

"The Delahuntys. The boy, Franklin, who caused the crash that killed Peter and Jack, along with his mother. I don't remember the mother's name. I broke into their home and murdered them both. I don't remember how I got into their house, but I killed them with a gun."

"You? What?" Jacob couldn't form a coherent sentence. What he was hearing was beyond his imagination. "You murdered the people involved in your car accident? Peter, please tell me you're lying."

"I'm not Peter, and I would appreciate it if you stopped referring to me as such. The Delahuntys needed to die, regardless of whose fault it was for the crash. Peter and Jack needed to be avenged. Franklin was a factor in their deaths. This was something I owed Peter in return for his body."

"You son of a bitch!"

"They tried to protest Franklin's innocence, and even said that it was Peter's fault, but I saw through their lies."

Jacob took all this in. He knew that Peter had died in a car accident, and that it had involved a teenage boy named Franklin Delahunty, but he only knew bare-bones details behind what had happened. Whether Peter or Franklin had caused the crash was beyond Jacob's knowledge, and he could only assume that if the kid wasn't in jail by now, then he must have been innocent.

Jacob remembered the copy of the autopsy report that he had gotten from Benjamin O'Toole. Benjamin had mentioned that it came with a few legal documents that he was required to sign when picking up Peter and Jack's bodies from the county coroner. When Jacob had looked over the autopsy report upon retrieving Peter's body, he didn't think much of it when he saw the arrest report stapled to the back. He had stuffed the report away in his research carelessly and forgot about it. It was the only explanation as to how Peter could have found out the full story behind how he died and where Franklin lived.

"My God, Peter." Jacob pressed his hand against his forehead. It felt like the world was spinning. "How could you?"

"Stop calling me Peter."

"Why are you referring to yourself in the third person?"

Peter coughed over the line, and then took a heavy breath. "I know who I am now. For a long time, I struggled to reconcile with this new form, but I've realized what I am. Peter Murphy is dead. He died in that car accident back in December. He has ceased to exist. Angela Fairhardt and Timothy Saunders have ceased to exist as well. What you created was not Peter, nor even Tim or Angela, but something else—a new form of life that has never walked on this planet before. I am not white, nor black. Not man, nor woman. Not alive or dead. I am a new evolution of the previous three human beings that make up aspects of my new form. The body we share is a vessel within which all three of us reside. I am not singularly Peter, Angela, or Tim. I am Peter-Tim-Angela, three retired beings evolved into a single new unnatural being."

None of what Peter was saying made any sense. Jacob's hand clutched the cushion next to him. "This is insanity."

"No, it's not. It's logically sound. Who are you to decide what I am?"

The Modern Prometheus

"I created you."

"That may be true, but it is not for you to decide what I am. You merely laid the framework for this new species of life form, and it is my duty in this new body to innovate upon it. You gave me existence, and I created essence."

Jacob closed his eyes and carefully thought over where he was going to take this conversation. "Listen to me, Peter. You've suffered multiple emotional and physical traumas in rapid succession. Not only this, but I think whatever is happening to your body is affecting your mind as well. I think you may be suffering from rapid cell death. That includes the nerve cells in your brain. Everything in your body is failing."

The line was quiet for a long time. "No," Peter said. His voice was a little shaken. "No, that's incorrect. You're wrong. My body is merely evolving, shedding its previous incarnations. I am developing a new consciousness."

"You're going to die, Peter. Your body is going to—"

"Shut your mouth!" Peter snapped. "You're just jealous. I am what you'll never become, and you're trying to get me to doubt myself, after I've come so close to discovering who I am and what potential I hold!"

He's in denial, Jacob thought. *He can't accept what he's become, so he's substituting his reality with something else. That's the only explanation. Tread cautiously with what you say next.*

"Whatever you think you've become is not possible," Jacob said. "I fear you may be falling into psychosis, not just because of the cell death, but also as a way to rationalize what's happened to you and what you've done. Most of your body and the entirety of your mind is still Peter Murphy. I think your reanimation is giving you a profound and destructive identity and existential crisis. Something like ego-death, the complete loss of subjective self-identity."

"Excuse me?" Peter laughed. "If anything, I know myself better now than I ever have."

"Peter, you are still *you*. You are still your mind, even if parts of your body are other people. Do you understand? You're just confused, that's all. You need to stop, do you hear me? You need to stop hurting people!"

"You said it yourself, Jacob. Sartre. Essence precedes existence. Existence precedes essence. We once were, and then we ceased to be. Now, we've become something else, and we are only just discovering our essence as one singular being, evolved from the natural to the unnatural. I am that being."

"You've gone completely crazy, Peter!"

"It only sounds crazy to someone who has never experienced this evolution themselves." Peter then sneeringly added, "And never will."

"You were a mistake, Peter. I never should have created you."

"I'm a mistake, and yet I'm still here. That doesn't sound like a mistake to me." Peter's labored breaths wheezed over the line. "I can feel them, you know. I can feel Peter, Timothy and Angela in my body. Most of all, though, I feel Peter. I can feel his pain and his needs. He no longer exists, but the sensations of him still haunt me. It's like…"

"A phantom limb?"

"Yes, a phantom limb. That's what Peter has become. Even though he is gone, I can still feel something of his—this phantom limb of mine. It's like a bond. I feel the love he had for his family. It makes me feel good, like… like an expectant mother. Fulfilled in a way that I'm not as I am now. When I dwell on these old feelings Peter possessed, I get all tingly, and filled with desire. I have decided on a course of action. I need your assistance."

"I'll never help you."

"I have ways of coercing you, Jacob. I know you're weak. Do you remember when I shoved my gun in your face? You squealed like a weasel. You're terrified of death. You told me yourself that the whole reason why I exist is because of that terror."

"Maybe there are worse things than death to be afraid of, especially now."

"If that's the case, then I have other ways of making you do what I want you to. I still have some of your research. I could expose it to the world. Maybe I could go to the Boston School of Medicine and show them everything in those folders and binders I took. It may not be all of your research, but it's enough of it for them to build on. I could even offer my body for examination and experimentation. I'll tell them the whole thing; about me, your cabin, and your experiments. It's certainly against the Hippocratic Oath, what you've done. The police will want to have a word with you, considering all the bribes, body-snatchings, and fraud. I have a lot of evidence in the few folders I took."

"You absolute monster."

"I am *not* a monster," Peter said testily. "You have no control over me. You *will* do what I tell you to, and this is what I want. Are you listening?"

"Fine."

"I am alone in the world. I have no place to go that will accept me. I have decided that I want other unnatural beings like myself to accompany me. I want a family, like what Peter had. Within me, I can feel my phantom limb's love and passion for his wife and remaining child, Marjorie and Erin. It makes me

The Modern Prometheus

envious. I crave that bond for myself, so I want Marjorie and Erin as my bride and child. I will bring about the cessation of their current forms of existence, deliver their bodies to you, and you will evolve them into the same unnatural species I am. They will not accept me in their current forms, so I will make them like myself."

"Peter—"

"I'm not finished. I believe they are staying with Peter's mother-in-law, Helena. It shouldn't take long for me to reach them. I will take care of my business with them and then proceed to the cabin with their retired forms from there. You will make them like me."

Jacob couldn't think of any intelligent response to this request. "I"—he kept stammering—"I won't."

"You will. You've already crossed the threshold, the point of no return. You can't stop now because there is no salvation for you. You owe me this."

"I physically cannot—"

"I'm not taking 'no' for an answer. You said yourself that you need the subjects to be as fresh as possible, so I will work quickly. If you need more subjects to replace any damage I've done to Erin and Marjorie's bodies, then I will provide you with more subjects. I will arrive either late tonight or tomorrow morning. Do not disappoint me, or I will make you feel pain you've never experienced before in your life. And if that won't sway you, then I'll make sure that the world knows what you've discovered."

The line clicked.

Enraged, Jacob slammed the phone receiver against the table until it broke. He hated his creation, but most of all he hated himself.

This was a colossal fuckup, and it was all Jacob's fault. He had no idea just how far this mistake would go. No longer could he wait for the cell degeneration in Peter's body to run its course, and he cursed himself for ever giving him the benefit of the doubt.

What if he's right? Jacob thought. *What if he really is no longer Peter Murphy?*

Don't play into his delusions. The crushing weight of his circumstances have driven him crazy, not to mention the fact that his brain is literally decomposing. Peter is consciously disassociating himself from everything, either to escape or to cope—maybe both. Why else would he want Marjorie and Erin as his "unnatural" and "evolved" bride and daughter? It's because he's still Peter, and he still has feelings for his family. He's crazy, and you need to put him down.

No more waiting, no more negotiations. No more spilled blood. Jacob went downstairs and into the makeshift bedroom that had been Peter's during his first month of life. The TV

Jacob had set up on a chair lay on the floor, and black shards from the screen were scattered about.

In a corner of the room, Jacob saw the syringe that he had filled with a deadly combination of pancuronium bromide, potassium chloride, and sodium thiopental. It had been knocked from his hand during his struggle with Peter the night of his escape. He took the syringe and held it to the light bulb hanging from the ceiling, eyeing the clear liquid within.

I'm complicit in the murders of the Delahuntys, he thought. *I may not have been the one to pull the trigger, but I created the circumstances that lead to their deaths. And now if I don't destroy Peter, a woman and her child will die. Possibly even more.*

Jacob swallowed, gripped the syringe tightly in his hand, and scurried out of the room.

38.

The murky motel room greeted Peter with its familiar rancid aroma. He turned on the light and saw Jacob's research lying on the table, still opened and spread out. The first thing he did was gather it all together in a neat pile. It would be useful leverage against Jacob and would be vital in bringing him the family he craved.

Peter looked down at his arms. The flesh had become loose and slippery, the complexion a sickly mixture of yellow and green. The rashes had become bleeding blisters, and his white T-shirt had become badly stained with pus and blood. All over his body he felt intense burning sensations, and within him were sharp pains and throbbing cramps. It was a reminder that he was still alive.

My body is transforming, he thought gleefully. *I'm changing, like a butterfly. All of Peter, Tim, and Angela are washing away and I am becoming my true form.*

The bandages on his head were becoming too much of a hassle. They were bloated with fluids and kept getting undone. No longer was he concerned with The Expression. Before, when he still believed that he was Peter Murphy, he was ashamed of himself, terrified to even gaze at his own reflection. There was nothing to be afraid anymore.

Peter sat down on the bed and began undoing the bandages. It was a liberating experience. Every loop he unraveled made him feel closer to himself. Flies began buzzing around his head like vultures, but Peter ignored them.

At one point, as he undid the wraps near the middle of his face, he felt something land in his lap. It was the bloody chunk of his nose. He ceased unwrapping for a moment, took the nose up in between two fingers, and examined it curiously.

Another artifact of the deceased Peter Murphy, he thought to himself, and then pitched it across the room. *He won't miss it.*

The bandages were finally off. Peter stood and dropped them to the floor and sucked in air through the remaining teeth in his mouth. He was free.

In the bathroom, shards of the mirror were still strewn all over the sink and floor. Peter knelt, took up one large shard, and held it up to his face to see himself. It was magnificent. Never had he looked so beautiful. His new features were coming in nicely. In many ways, he felt sorry for Peter Murphy, who could never in his dreams attain this sort of evolutionary triumph.

Peter dropped the mirror shard and stepped out of the bathroom. He sat on the bed and turned on the old TV. It flickered to life, and after Peter smacked the side of it a few times, the reception cleared. He flipped through channels until he found the local news station, and he watched until what he was looking for came on.

"HOME INVASION AND DOUBLE MURDER IN METHUEN" appeared in big letters across the screen. A shot of the Delahunty residence appeared, and its driveway was lined with yellow tape. Several police officers stood on the front lawn, chatting with each other or speaking into their radios.

A blonde female news anchor named Stacy Whitman stood across the street from the property with a microphone in her hand. "The city of Methuen is in shock this afternoon after the bodies of nineteen-year-old Franklin Delahunty and his mother, forty-four-year-old Cynthia, were discovered early this morning by a neighbor."

Peter leaned forward and knitted his hands together tightly between his knees. *Ah, Cynthia*, he thought. *That's what her name was.*

"At around one o'clock this morning, a neighbor, who wishes to remain anonymous, was woken up by the sound of screams and gunshots from the Delahunty residence. Upon stepping outside to investigate, he saw a man wearing a white T-shirt and, quote, 'some kind of mask' run out the front door. He reports that the suspect was heard getting into a vehicle, then he saw a black truck, possibly a recent Ford model, speed out of the neighborhood. The neighbor claims that he did not have enough time to see the full license plate number, but states that the first three letters and numbers were '5WF.'"

Footage from earlier in the morning played. Men wearing latex gloves and dark blue coats with "ESSEX COUNTY CORONER" inscribed on the backs carried a body bag on a gurney down the front stoop, then wheeled it across the lawn to a big white van.

The news story then cut to a police officer with a big gray moustache. The caption at the bottom read "SGT. GENE SACRAMONI".

"It was very tragic," Sergeant Sacramoni reported, his voice steady. "The kid and his mom—it looked like whoever did this beat them. It doesn't look like anything was stolen, so the intent is likely murder."

The story then went back to Stacy again standing across the street from the property. "Essex County authorities are urging the public of Methuen and any surrounding communities to please keep an eye open for any rental black Ford truck with '5WF' on the license plates. The suspect is armed and dangerous, so please keep your distance and do not try to stop him yourself."

Peter shut off the TV. He didn't have much time. He had one advantage: any fingerprints or other biological evidence left at the crime scene would lead directly to a dead man. The truck, however, had to get taken care of. He grabbed all of Jacob's research and left the room.

The truck was parked in the back of the lot, hidden in the shade away from the check-in building. There were few other cars in the lot. The only one that wasn't near the check-in building was a gray van parked about five yards away. That would do just fine.

Peter opened the passenger door of the truck and slipped Jacob's research under the seat. He took his pocketknife and undid the screws on the front and back plates with it, and then stuffed the plates under the driver seat. Quickly, he jogged over to the van, unfastened the screws securing its plates, and took them.

This will buy me some time, he thought.

Peter returned to the truck and screwed the stolen plates on the front and back, tightening them in place with the tip of the knife. Even if the truck make, model, and color were identifiable, the change in plates would possibly throw the police off just a little bit. All he needed to do was get close to Helena's house, and then he could dump the truck and use her car from then on.

Everything is under control, Peter thought as he climbed into the driver seat. There was no need to check-out since he didn't want to draw any more attention to himself. It was best to just slip out of the motel quietly.

39.

The Murphy house looked like any other house in the neighborhood, but understanding the connotations attached to it made it seem to stand out more than the others. It was like there was some dark cloud surrounding the property that existed nowhere else nearby.

The driveway was empty. This was a relief, but it was also concerning. Jacob would not face Peter here, but it also meant that Peter was several steps ahead of him. He noted the tire marks in the driveway that ran from the front of the house to the street. Someone left in a hurry. He pulled in and got out, looking up at the second-floor windows. The evening sun trickled its light over the edge of the roof.

Where did you go, Peter?

Jacob remembered the address to this house, because he had driven by it the day he had picked up Peter's body from the funeral home. The funeral home was only a few streets away from the neighborhood, and Jacob had driven past the Murphy property out of curiosity before he met with Benjamin.

There were many things to consider. Peter was armed, and Jacob only had a syringe. If he was going to kill Peter, then he needed to be a little crafty—it was a matter of figuring out exactly where he was going. Jacob hoped that somehow, he could find a clue in Peter's old house. The only lead he had was the name of Peter's mother-in-law, Helena.

Jacob entered the house. It looked like an earthquake had hit it. Jacob imagined that Peter had ripped everything apart after finding out what he had become. A twinge of guilt jabbed his heart, but Jacob remained composed. Lives were at stake. He needed to focus.

What the hell could he find that would help him find Peter in this mess? Jacob walked around the living room, turning over furniture and picking up trash, finding absolutely nothing practical.

He decided to try the bedrooms. There had to be something personal in one of them that could lead to Helena. One bedroom looked like a toddler's room, and everything was packed up in boxes nice and neat. It must have been Jack's room. The bedroom across from Jack's room had pink sheets on the bed and little girls' clothes in the drawers, which meant that it had to have been Erin's. Numerous crude paintings with an easel were set in the closet, and it looked like several personal belongings were missing. Peter had mentioned that Erin was staying with Helena, so she must have taken a couple of things with her.

From what Jacob could tell, every room in the house had been trashed and ripped apart by Peter, except for the bedrooms of his two children. This made Jacob see a bigger picture that he had never considered before. Before, Jacob had only read about the Murphy family in files. Now, he was seeing where they lived, slept, played, and loved. It made Peter far more human than he had seemed before. It made him—

Don't think about that right now, Jacob told himself. *You need to focus. You have to MOVE.*

Jacob tried the room at the end of the hall and found what must have been Peter and Marjorie's bedroom. Jacob began opening drawers, throwing around clothes and old junk, trying to find anything that could give him a clue.

Come on, come on. Jacob was sweating. *Give me something!*

A knocked over basket next to the bedside table caught his attention. Several old envelopes and sheets of paper had spilled out of it. Jacob knelt and began sifting through it. It looked like a letter bin where either Marjorie or Peter kept all their old mail.

There were letters from the funeral home, a grossly expensive bill from Holy Family Hospital, parent-teacher conference notifications from Timberlane Middle School, among dozens of trivial bills. And then he found what he was looking for: an envelope and birthday card from Helena Strauss for Marjorie from the previous October. The return address read, "14 PISCATAQUOG STREET, MANCHESTER, NH, 03101".

Jacob gripped the card envelope hard in his fingers. *This is it. This is where Peter is going. I've got to beat him there.*

Jacob stood and stuffed the envelope into his pocket, then rushed out of the house and got back into his car. He pulled out of the driveway and drove down Argyle Street, going ten miles over the residential speed limit.

A police cruiser appeared at the intersection at the end of the street, and Jacob nearly slammed on the brakes, but he refrained and instead slowed the car down to a legal ten miles an hour. It was an Atkinson police cruiser. It halted at the stop sign, then crossed the intersection onto Argyle and passed Jacob's car. Jacob stopped at the intersection and watched the cruiser go up the street in his rearview mirror. It turned into the driveway of the Murphy house. Two officers lumbered out, went up the stoop, and rang the doorbell.

Jesus Christ, what good timing. Jacob sighed. *But what are the police doing at the Murphy house?*

Did Peter already strike again?

Jacob didn't even want to consider it. He swallowed to wet his dry throat, then took a right at the intersection and left the neighborhood.

40.

Manchester was only a half-hour drive from Salem, if the traffic was merciful. All Peter needed to do was make it past the first five exits on I-93, merge onto I-293, and then finally pull off on Exit 5. That would take him near Elm Street, close to where Helena's neighborhood was.

Peter kept the truck cruising at a steady sixty-five miles an hour, as he didn't want to attract any cops looking for speeders. He was terrified but also excited, and to keep himself motivated he fantasized of his future wife and child. He imagined the moment they come to, awakening in this world just as he had.

Only unlike him, they wouldn't be alone. He would console them and love them in ways he hadn't been when he was reborn. He would hold them, kiss them, tell them everything was all right, and then congratulate them on their transformation.

Already, he was brainstorming places they could go to start anew—perhaps the deserts of Arizona, the sprawling plains of Wyoming, or even the mountains of Northern California. Somewhere far away from normal humans so they could live in peace. Maybe they could even make more specimens like themselves and create their own little colony of evolved humans. All sorts of possibilities opened in Peter's mind, and he had to fight with himself to keep from going above the minimum speed limit. It was all just so thrilling, and he didn't want to wait longer than he had to.

My beautiful bride, he kept thinking. *My beautiful child. All three of us together.*

He was so enchanted by his fantasy that it wasn't until the lights of a state trooper's cruiser began flashing that he realized he was being tailed. Its blue lights blared so brightly that it lit up the inside of his truck in the coming evening dark.

There was nothing to be afraid of. Normal humans didn't frighten him. Carefully, Peter slowed the truck down, pulled over to the side of the interstate, and stopped. He drew the gun from his pants and sat back in his seat, watching the driver side mirror.

The trooper got out of his cruiser, adjusted his campaign hat, and approached the truck. His hand was on his holster. The sound of his shoes clunking against the pavement grew louder as he approached.

"Sir, I need you to—"

The trooper's sentence cut short the moment he saw Peter. Peter watched as the trooper's eyes widened in disbelief and awe. He was a young kid, probably in his early twenties, was clean-shaven and without a wrinkle in his smooth skin. Peter lifted the gun and shot him in the stomach.

The trooper yelped and staggered back. Peter shoved the door open as the trooper fled to his cruiser, clutching his abdomen. Peter shot at the trooper just as he yanked the driver's door open. The bullet hit the windshield, and a huge, shattered star appeared in the glass like cracked ice. The trooper peeked out from behind the door and fired off a few shots back. Peter ran around to the front of the truck and took cover, clutching his gun to his chest.

When no follow-up shot came, Peter peeked around the truck. The trooper was leaning inside his cruiser, screaming into the mouthpiece of his dashboard radio. Peter popped out and pulled the trigger three times. One shot hit the fender, the other didn't seem to hit anything, but the third bullet went through the windshield, creating another star-shaped crack in it. The trooper squealed in agony.

Peter kept the gun aimed at the windshield, and he performed a slice-the-pie maneuver around the cruiser. A big van on the interstate laid on its horn, and then sped past him, the driver apparently seeing what was unfolding. The radio inside the cruiser was screeching, "Parkland! Parkland, what the fuck is happening, buddy? Answer me!"

The trooper was laying over the driver seat and middle armrest, both smeared with blood, with his arm crossed over his chest and stomach. His face was gray, and his lips were blue. He reached down to try and grab his gun from where it lay around the pedals. The look in his eyes reminded Peter of the look Franklin had given him before he killed him.

"Wait," the trooper managed. "I'm scared."

Peter fired. He had been aiming at the trooper's face, but he must not have been holding the gun tight enough, because the shot hit him in the neck. Blood gushed out of his destroyed throat, and it poured into the seat and to the floor.

The radio kept blaring, "Brian! Jesus Christ, say something, man!"

Peter trotted back to his truck, climbed in, and took off.

41.

Dusk fell on Lowell. Lights were on in the little houses that lined the narrow pothole-strewn street that was Union Avenue. The hushed voices of people within the houses could be heard as they had dinner or gathered in their living rooms to settle in for the day.

Owen Murphy turned onto Union Avenue with a fresh twelve-pack in his hand. He walked with an inebriated swagger, as he had been going hard all day, hitting bottle after bottle, can after can, until the whole world didn't have him by the throat so much. The only reason he had gone out was because he ran out of booze, and he had reluctantly decided to take the fifteen-minute walk to the gas station a few streets away to get more. He'd need it. If he didn't have it, he would think too much about that dream he had a few nights ago.

The duplex he lived in came into view, and Owen stepped onto the front porch. He struggled to find the doorknob for a few moments before finally getting a grip on it, and then he stepped inside. He'd long since stopped caring about locking his front door anymore, even after a break-in he'd experienced a few years back. In fact, part of him hoped that some intruder would come in and blow his brains out. Lord knew that he was too cowardly to do it himself. He didn't have anything valuable for them to steal anyway.

Owen nearly tripped on an empty bottle in the foyer, but caught himself on the wall, gripping the fresh pack of beer in his hand like a delicate diamond he didn't want to drop. Once he regained his balance, he managed to make it to the kitchen, where he set the beer on the table and sat down.

Now this party could resume. He opened the pack, dug a can out, and popped it open, his ears savoring the *psssst* sound it made. It went down smooth as he chugged it. His vision swam, but he didn't care. The last thing he wanted to see clearly was his filthy kitchen, which he hadn't cleaned in months. Maybe after a few more months, he could collect all the bottles and cans and get them recycled for more booze money.

Drinking had been a consistent thing since his brother and nephew died. The question kept nagging him after the funeral: "What's the point?" What *was* the point, to refrain from what he wanted to do? He wanted to drink and be as far away from what happened as possible. He couldn't bear to face it completely in full clarity. It scared him, so he drank, and he hadn't stopped for six months now. Owen was sure his brother was watching him from wherever he was now, disappointed.

Owen took another big pull of his beer and finished it off. He crushed it in his fist, chucked it over his shoulder, and dug another one out of the pack.

Especially after that dream he had of Peter, he needed to drink. It must have been a dream. The most that Owen could remember was passing out in the very kitchen he sat in now, and he awoke delirious to see his dead brother standing in the doorway. It was terrifying and confusing. Owen knew that it had been his brother—he recognized his voice, his figure, his face—and yet he looked strange. There was something not quite right with his face. Peter had said something to him, but Owen couldn't for the life of him remember what it had been. He only remembered getting enraged, then sobbing his eyes out, and then waking up shortly afterward, alone again.

That dream had followed him since, invading his thoughts, making him feel things he tried to push away as hard as he could. It had almost seemed real, like he had seen the ghost of his dead brother right in his own home. It disturbed him so much that he had even tried calling his sister-in-law to tell her about it. However, she wouldn't pick up, so Owen had drunkenly called her mother, Helena. He couldn't recall what he had told her over the phone, and frankly he didn't want to. It was embarrassing to think about.

Owen popped open the fresh can and downed three quarters of the beer almost in one gulp. He set it on the table with a hollow metallic *clank* and exhaled. This was what he needed. No, he wouldn't think about that dream anymore, at least not for a while. He wouldn't think about Peter or little Jackie, either. He just wanted to hide away in this house and fall into his black pit.

Just as he raised the beer to his lips to finish it off, a hard knock came against his front door. Owen blinked, surprised and not entirely sure if what he was hearing was real. Then the knock came again, harder this time, and he knew someone was at the door for sure.

"Hold on!" he called, and then finished the beer. Again, he crushed the can and pitched it over his shoulder, then got up, staggered into the foyer, and opened the front door.

Two Lowell police officers stood on his front porch, their thumbs hooked in their belts, looking at Owen with stony faces. One was short and pudgy, and the other was tall with red bushy hair and a long, wooden face. The name tag of the pudgy one read, "DUFRESNE", and the tag of the red haired one read, "JONES."

"Uhh," Owen uttered.

"Are you Owen Murphy?" Dufresne said.

"Yeah, that's me."

"Do you mind if we ask you a few questions?"

Owen raised an eyebrow. "What's the matter, officers?"

"I think it would be best if you invited us in to have a talk."

Owen figured that he didn't have anything to hide anyway, and even if he did, he didn't care. He stepped out of the way and let the officers in.

All three shuffled into the kitchen. Owen sat at the table while the two cops stood, flanking him from the front and to his right. Jones looked around and whistled at the mess all over the table, counters, and floor.

"May we ask where you were earlier today at around four o'clock?" Dufresne said.

Owen shrugged, dug out another beer, and opened it. "I was here. Drinking."

"Do you drive at all, sir?"

"I don't have any car. Don't need one. I used to walk to work, but now I don't work anymore. I don't go anywhere, don't do anything. I like it that way."

The two cops looked at each other. Owen drank his beer in a single gulp, crushed it, pitched it, and then exhaled.

"We can't help but notice that you haven't asked us why we're speaking to you, Mr. Murphy," Dufresne said.

Owen held his hands up in flippant indifference. "If the cops wanna talk to me, sure I'll talk to them. Whatever. You gonna bust me for drinking in the privacy of my own home?"

Jones finally spoke up. "Have you heard about what happened in Methuen last night?"

"I haven't heard anything. Haven't even turned on the TV."

"A mother and her teenage kid were found dead in their home. They were beaten and then murdered with gunshot wounds to the head. The names might be familiar to you. Franklin and Cynthia Delahunty."

Owen had reached out to grab another beer from the pack but stopped himself the moment he heard the name "Franklin Delahunty." That name. Just hearing it again made the hairs on his arms and the back of his neck stand erect. All sorts of emotions flooded into his chest, and quickly he grabbed another beer and opened it.

"They were murdered?" he asked.

"That's right. Based on how they died, it is believed that it was premeditated murder, and that Franklin was the primary target," Dufresne said.

"We understand that Franklin Delahunty was involved in a car crash that killed your brother and nephew back around Christmas."

"Yeah." Owen's voice was faint.

"Franklin was arrested for their deaths, but after an investigation by the state police and highway division, it was discovered that he did not cause the crash. Your brother caused the crash. And now Franklin is dead. A targeted murder."

There was no concrete way for Owen to feel about this. He understood from a logical standpoint that there was no reason for him to resent Franklin Delahunty, but he *had* been involved in the deaths of Peter and Jack. Owen knew that it was unfair to blame Franklin, but hearing that he and his mother had been murdered only complicated his feelings.

"So, somebody killed them, huh." Owen sipped his beer.

"That's right," Dufresne said. "And somebody has been using your sister-in-law's debit card."

Owen suddenly sobered up. "What?"

Jones explained: "A neighbor of the Delahunty's spotted a suspect leaving their residence around the time of the murders. A man wearing something on his face and a T-shirt. He got into a black Ford truck with the first three letters of the plates being '5WF,' but the witness wasn't able to get any more details than that."

"What's this have to do with me or my sister-in-law?"

"At the Rockingham Motel in Salem, a witness staying there saw the news story this afternoon and reported that he had seen a black Ford truck with '5WF-99HR' on its plates around the parking lot. By the time he told the front desk, the truck had already left. A Salem police officer investigated and found that a pair of New Hampshire plates had been stolen off a vehicle on the property. The lady working check-in said that a funny looking guy with nasty rashes all over his face driving a black truck had stayed a few nights at the motel."

Jones paused for a moment to examine Owen's face and body language, which was oblivious and shocked. He continued, "The lady said that it was a Ford Heritage, possibly from the early 2010s. The suspect was using Marjorie Murphy's debit card—your sister-in-law."

Owen reclined in his seat. He felt as if he had just gotten punched in the face. Even heavily under the influence, the information he had just been given scared him shitless. "What does all this mean?" he asked.

"It means that Franklin Delahunty may have made an enemy in your family. The fact that the prime suspect in the murders is using your widowed sister-in-law's debit card backs this up."

"I'm not a suspect, am I?"

"We'd like to keep asking you questions, if you don't mind, Mr. Murphy."

Dufresne stepped forward. "Mr. Murphy, a few police officers in Atkinson arrived at your sister-in-law's home today to question her about her card. There were no vehicles in the driveway, and nobody answered the door. Do you know where she is?"

"She's uh"—Owen struggled to remember details from the conversation he had had with Helena. *God damn it, why was I so drunk when I did that?*

Just then, the radio on the pudgy cop's shoulder crackled, "Officer Dufresne?"

"Yes, I'm here," Dufresne answered. He nodded at Jones and then stepped out of the kitchen.

Jones set his hands firmly on the table and looked down at Owen. "Where is your sister-in-law, Mr. Murphy?"

Owen remembered. "She's with her mother, Helena Strauss. I tried calling her a few times, but she didn't answer her phone. I called Helena this morning to ask her about where she might be, because I was getting worried. She said that Margie was staying with her in Manchester. My niece is there too, Erin is her name."

Dufresne stepped back into the kitchen with his arms loose at his sides. He had a blank, flabbergasted look on his face.

"What?" Jones said.

"They just told me over the radio—a New Hampshire trooper was shot to death on I-93. He stopped a Ford Heritage with New Hampshire plates just past Exit 3. The last thing he radioed was that he was being attacked by some deformed crazy fuck with a gun. A few other troopers just now arrived on the scene and found him dead. The perp got away, going north."

"What the fuck is going on?" Owen cried. "Is my sister-in-law okay? Who is this guy?"

Jones swooped in and jabbed a finger at Owen's face. "Where did you say this Helena lady was?"

"She's in Manchester. I don't know the exact address because I wasn't close to her, but she's not far from Elm Street. The street name starts with a 'P,' and it sounds Native American."

"Scott," Jones looked at the Dufresne, "get Manchester on the horn. Tell them to find the residence of Helena Strauss. It looks like the suspect may be going there."

Owen stood. "What's happening? Please tell me Margie and Erin are gonna be okay."

"You stay right here," Dufresne ordered. "We'll be right back. Got it?"

The two cops rushed out of the kitchen. The front door was heard opening and slamming shut, followed by the heavy footfalls of the officers as they stepped off the porch.

Owen was experiencing the worst kind of panic: drunken panic. He lurched around the kitchen until he found his phone on the counter by the sink. He took it up and again tried to call his sister-in-law. Impatiently, he listened to the ringing over the line.

"Pick up, for Christ's sake, Margie!"

The ringing ceased, and someone answered.

"Margie!" Owen shouted. "You finally fucking picked up! Are you okay? What's happening?"

Someone was breathing on the other end of the line, heavy and pained breaths. And then they chuckled—a familiar chuckle.

Owen slammed his fist on the counter, rattling the empty bottles and cans on it. "Who is this? Who the fuck is this?"

"Do you recognize my voice, Owen?" the stranger said.

Owen felt his heart drop into his stomach. He did recognize the voice.

The line went dead. Owen stood with his phone pressed to his ear, unable to comprehend what he had just experienced. His thoughts turned back to the dream he had a few nights before, and he suddenly realized that it hadn't been a dream at all.

The phone dropped from his hand, and Owen tumbled to the floor like a collapsing tree. He fainted.

42.

Pulling off on Exit 5 of I-293, Peter entered Manchester and immediately pulled into a parking lot on Commercial Street along the Merrimack River, near the University of New

The Modern Prometheus

Hampshire's Manchester campus. He was going to have to ditch the truck and move on foot.

Before he got out, he checked the magazine of his pistol. Two bullets left, plus one still in the chamber. It was more than enough if he was careful. He slid the magazine back into the gun and got out of the vehicle.

Late evening had fallen on the city. The streetlights were on, and the blinding glare of car headlights went up and down Commercial Street. Peter crossed at an intersection, went up a block, and then made his way down Elm Street towards the SNHU Arena. His destination was no more than a twenty-minute walk away.

A bar with neon lights hanging in the windows was ahead. A man stood at a meter digging in his pocket for change. A young couple stumbled out of the bar with cigarettes in their hands, laughing and kissing each other. They slipped their cigarettes into their mouths, pressed the tips together, and the man dug out a lighter and lit them both at the same time.

As Peter came up the sidewalk, the man at the meter saw him just as he was sticking a quarter in. He leapt back and shouted, "Jesus Christ!"

The young couple, alerted by the exclamation, turned and saw Peter next. The woman shrieked and covered her face, dropping her cigarette to the ground, which landed in a little flurry of orange sparks. The man she was with took a step back and all color drained from his face. The cigarette in his mouth bounced as his lips searched for a way to express his horror.

Pay them no mind, Peter told himself as he passed them. *They'll never understand.*

It was true. They *would* never understand. He knew what he had become was awe-inspiring. He heard their feet clap against the sidewalk as they ran away, shouting for help.

43.

To Margie's surprise, Erin came into the living room with a board game box in her hands, and her little eyes—which looked so much like Peter's—peeked over the top of it.

"Wanna play?" she said.

Margie smiled and turned off the TV. Erin must have gotten the board game from the closet, which was filled with them. Those games had been an old recreational activity that the family engaged in whenever they visited Grandma Helena. Erin had grown to resent them as she got older.

"I thought you hated those games, Erin."

Erin shrugged and set the board game on the coffee table. "Well, I wanna play one."

"Of course we can play." Margie looked over her shoulder to the kitchen, where Helena was filling a pot of water in the sink. "Hey Mom, you wanna play a game with us?"

"Maybe not at this moment, sweetheart. I've got to get dinner on. I was caught up in something and didn't even think about it until now. You go right on ahead. I might join in later."

Margie got off the couch and knelt on the floor at one end of the coffee table, and Erin sat at the other end. She opened the box and set up the board and game pieces.

"You still remember how to play this one?" Margie asked.

"Yeah, I do. It's been a long time, though."

"Want me to read the rulebook again?"

"Okay."

Helena placed the pot on the stove and turned one of the dials. It would take a few minutes for the water to boil, so she dug out a bag of potatoes from under the counter and began peeling them. Mashed potatoes tonight seemed all right.

As she peeled, she could hear her granddaughter and daughter laughing, reminiscing about old times. "Remember when you caught Dad cheating when he skipped a few spaces ahead?" Margie asked.

"Yeah, I was mad about that!" Erin replied. "I took the game board and hit him over the head with it."

"Are you gonna do that to me?"

"You're not gonna try and cheat, are you?"

"Maybe I will. And if I do, you'll have to catch me."

"You're on, nerd."

Helena smiled. It was nice, hearing them bond like this. It had been too long since she could remember them getting along. She peeked into the living room at them. Erin reached over the board and tried grabbing a card off the stack in the middle of the table, and Margie quickly nabbed the stack out of her reach. "I don't think so!" she said and laughed. Erin got up and tried to grab a card from the pile, but Margie held it away from her.

"Okay, okay, settle down!" Margie said. "I'll give you your cards when you get to the space that says you can take one. We're never going to get started at this rate."

Erin giggled mischievously and returned to her spot. Margie began shuffling the cards.

A sharp pain crossed Helena's thumb. She realized that she had accidentally drawn the blade over her finger. She set the knife down and uttered a quiet gasp. Sucking on her finger, she slipped out of kitchen and went into the bathroom to grab a band aid from the medicine cabinet.

Through the window, she could hear a helicopter. Its propeller buzzed in the distance, grew louder as it passed over the house, then went quiet as it flew away. Helena listened to it curiously as she wrapped the band aid around her finger. Being in a city, it wasn't uncommon to hear helicopters or anything like that, but Manchester wasn't a big metropolis by any means. A helicopter circling around that low overhead usually only happened when a shooting or some other horrible crime had occurred and the perpetrator was still out there.

Sighing, Helena closed the cabinet. *This city sure has gone down the drain since the eighties,* she thought.

It looked like Margie and Erin had finally gotten the game started. Erin jiggled a pair of dice in her cupped hands, and then dropped them to the table. "Five spaces," she said.

"Bullshit," Margie said, leaning over to look. "That's a one and a three. Behave yourself, kiddo."

"Fine." Erin moved four spaces. "Hey Grandma, why don't you play with us?"

"I gotta get the potatoes ready, Erin," Helena said. "Give it a little while, and maybe—"

A knock sounded against the front door—three consecutive knocks, then a pause, followed by three harder knocks. Margie and Helena looked at each other.

"Honey, are you expecting anyone?" Helena asked.

"No?"

"Keep playing your game. I'll answer."

The front door had a peephole, but when Helena looked through it, all she saw was black. Strange. She unlocked it, but kept the chain on, then opened the door about two inches. Through the opening, a lidless and inflamed eyeball gaped at her. Labored hot breath blew against her face through the rotting teeth of a lipless mouth, and it stank of death and rot. Blood ran down a leathery balding scalp. The mummified face grinned at her.

"Hello, Helena," it said.

The monster reached through the opening with one gangrenous claw-like hand. Helena shrieked and backed away.

Margie and Erin stood just as the living corpse slammed through the door, snapping the chain off the wall. It staggered into the living room and looked at Margie. She saw the single blue eye in its horrible face. She recognized it, and all at once she felt cold dread shoot through her body.

"Darling," it said.

Erin latched onto her leg. "Mom—Mom?"

The corpse slammed the front door shut and drew a gun from its pants. Margie knew that it was the same gun that Peter had bought after his brother got robbed. One moment, she was playing an innocent board game with her daughter, and then the next she was looking at the living cadaver of her husband with a gun aimed at her.

"Get on the floor!" it shouted. Its voice was slurred, barely able to enunciate words with its ravished mouth. "Get down and be quiet!"

Margie and Erin fell to the floor, holding each other. Helena lunged forward, but the monster then pointed its gun at her.

"Don't try it, Helena," it said. "Get down with them. Now."

Helena moved but tripped over the carpet and fell to the floor. She crawled over to where her daughter and granddaughter were huddled together and got in front of them, holding her arms out. Their horrified and bewildered faces looked up at the beast.

The creature stared at them. It seemed like it was suffering just trying to stand up straight and breathe. It sucked in air, and then exhaled in a long wheeze, sounding like a whistle as it passed what few teeth were left in its mouth. The expression in its ruined face could not be understood. The skin was leathery and seemed to sag off the front of its skull. Half of its face was decomposed. One of its eyes looked partially deflated and hung loose in red tissue within a cavernous socket. Its nose was missing, and only two narrow triangular holes leaking mucus with some cartilage remained. Below the loose eye, the cheek was decomposed, and the teeth, gums and jaw could be seen. Wet white maggots squirmed in and out of the flesh that remained around the cheek. Flies buzzed around its head like locusts.

The monster took in more air, spat away some of the maggots, and composed itself. "Margie, Erin," it said. Its words were elongated and pained, as if even just speaking were an exhausting and agonizing endeavor. "Just look at what Peter has become. Isn't it wonderful?"

Margie wrapped her arms around her daughter's head and pulled her face into her chest. "It's not—no, it can't—"

"It is."

Margie screamed.

"Make it stop!" Erin cried.

"Leave my family alone!" Helena shouted.

The corpse knelt in front of Helena and aimed its gun at her face. "Move, Helena. This is not your business."

"I don't know what you are, but you won't hurt my family."

"Move!"

Helena grabbed its face, wanting to claw whatever tender flesh there was left off. The creature stood and grabbed at her hands. Helena's fingernails dug into its juicy skin with ease, and for a moment it revolted her enough to want to stop, but she kept going. Helena got up with it, trying to get her thumbs in its eye sockets.

The monster whipped the pistol across Helena's face. Helena staggered back, grabbing her forehead, and the corpse lunged forward and tackled her to the ground.

"Mom!" Margie got up and leapt on the creature's back, hitting it in the side of the head. With every thwack, she felt the cold, wet, spongy skin of its face. The monster thrust its head back, hitting Margie in the nose, and she fell off to the ground.

"Mom!" Erin crawled over to her mother, who grabbed her bleeding nose.

The corpse pinned Helena to the floor by her neck. "You never did appreciate Peter, you old miserable fucking spinster." It drew a pocketknife and began stabbing her in the chest. Helena screamed and flailed her arms around, hitting her attacker's chest and face. Her hand pressed against its mouth, and she felt her finger push one of its few remaining teeth into its mouth.

"Oh my God, help me!" she screamed.

Margie propped herself on her elbows and watched as the monster stabbed her mother to death. It drew the knife up, clenched in a feminine hand, and then brought it down into her chest. Helena's screams became gargles as blood oozed from her mouth and her eyes rolled into the back of her head. Then, she stopped struggling and lay flat on the floor.

Margie clutched her daughter, who was sobbing hysterically. The monster grabbed the gun from where it had fallen near the couch. It stood over Helena's corpse and dropped the knife. Covered in Helena's blood, the creature turned to Margie and pointed the gun at her. Its tongue slithered between its gums, then it spat out the tooth that Helena had knocked loose.

"What are you?" Margie pleaded. It was the only thing her mind could compel her to say.

The creature knelt in front of her, "I brought Peter to see you again, in his new, evolved form. Peter is dead, Margie. I am a new being that was born from Peter, Timothy and Angela."

"Oh God, Peter, what are you talking about?"

"I can feel Peter's love for you and your daughter inside of me, and I've come to make you both mine. Do you miss Peter?"

"Peter," she whispered hoarsely, "every day I wish I could have done or said something that kept you and Jack off the road that night. I think about you and Jack every day. I told myself that I wanted you back. I'm sorry, okay? I'm sorry that I didn't do anything to save you and our son! Just please don't kill us. Please."

"Make it go away! I don't want to die!" Erin cried into her mother's chest. "Why do you want to kill us, Daddy?"

"I know that it's scary," it said gently. Its breath stank of the grave, and it spat out more maggots to the floor. "But there is no such thing as death. I'm here to reunite you and your mother with your father. Your father lives on in me. Don't you want that?"

Erin dug her fingernails into her mother so hard that Margie could feel her drawing blood.

"We'll be together." The monster reached its feminine hand out to Erin. "Once the messy part is over with, we'll be a family."

Its fingertips tickled Erin's hair, and Erin tore herself away from her mother and crawled away.

The monster stood and grunted. "Don't you turn away from me," it said.

Erin made it to the wall on the other side of the room and pressed her back against it, staring at the creature with her eyes wide open.

"Not like the others," it said, aiming the gun at her. "You will not turn me away like everyone else! You'll be with me forever!"

"Leave my daughter alone, you fuck!" Margie leapt and threw herself at the gun, but it was too late. Just as she grabbed the monster's arm, the gun fired. Margie and the creature fell onto the couch, and she rolled off onto the floor and looked at her daughter.

Erin clutched her neck. Blood spewed between her fingers, getting all over her clothes, the wall, and hardwood floor.

"Erin!" Margie flew to her daughter and rested her against her lap. Blood covered her pants and shirt. The little girl struggled to speak, choked, and whimpered. Margie pressed her hand against the wound, hopelessly trying to stop the bleeding. It was all to no avail. Within moments, Erin's eyes faded, and she stared lifelessly at the ceiling.

"Don't cry, Margie," the monster said. It managed to get off the couch and back on its feet. "She'll be with me now. You will too."

Margie said nothing. She held her dead daughter in her lap, her hands still pressed against her bloody neck. She looked up at the creature that was her late husband, her eyes like windows peering into an empty room. Consciousness cracked and faded as her mind disassociated from what was happening.

"Both of you. You'll be my wife and child. Once you've evolved like me, you'll have nowhere else to go. The world will reject you, just as it has with me, and you'll have no choice but to come to me. You *will* come to me. You'll be mine, and we'll be happy together. I promise."

The monster aimed its gun at her. Margie saw smoke still smoldering from the barrel. Her blank mind acknowledged it, as well as the creature's intentions, but she did not resist. She took a moment to look at her dead daughter and accepted it. She closed her eyes, turned her head away and waited.

The shot did not come. Instead, she heard struggling. Margie opened her eyes and saw a young man with blonde hair and big glasses locking his arm around the creature's neck from behind. It threw its arms out and jerked its head back, trying to get the intruder off.

"Stop struggling, Peter," the young man said.

"Get off me, Jacob! Get the fuck off me!"

The monster reached around with the gun and fired off a shot, but it missed and hit one of Erin's framed paintings on the wall. The glass in the frame cracked and the painting fell to the floor.

"No!" the creature squealed. "Get off! You can't do this! I'm so close, Jacob! Stop!"

The man named Jacob managed to get the monster on its knees. It dropped the pistol and grabbed at Jacob's arm. Jacob produced a syringe from his coat and jabbed it into the corpse's neck. The monster hollered as Jacob thumbed the plunger of the syringe.

"No, Jacob!" it pleaded. "Not yet! We need to be together! *WE NEED TO BE TOGETHER!*"

Jacob tore the syringe out of the monster's jugular and threw it away, then locked both of his arms around its neck. He managed to get it lying down flat against the floor, and he put all his weight on it. The creature dug its fingertips into the floor, ripping what few nails it had left out as it tried to crawl away. It sobbed and whined like some sad dog, and then the sobs turned into gags as foam bubbled out of its mouth. It fell into convulsions.

"Shh, Peter," Jacob said. "Just let it go."

"I can't—I don't—"

"Shhh. Let it go."

"I don't... *I don't want to be alone.*"

Within a minute, the monster stopped moving. Its blue eye—the one Margie recognized as her dead husband's—was fixated on her as life left it. Then, it was gone.

Jacob got off the monster. He looked at Margie. Utter devastation crossed his face as he examined her and the dead girl in her lap. His mouth quivered and his eyes glassed over.

"I'm so sorry," was the only thing he said. Then he turned on his heel and fled out through the front door. Moments later, a car engine started, and headlights shined through the windows, blinding Margie. The lights turned, and the car sped away into the night. Then, there was silence.

Margie looked down at her dead daughter. She ran her fingertips along Erin's cheek, smearing blood against it. She pulled Erin's face against hers and began to cry. She moaned her daughter's name again and again. The crying turned into hysterical wails, and her wails then became insane laughter.

So profound was her grieving that she hadn't heard the police sirens approaching the house. So intense was her trauma that she didn't notice two officers storming into the house, pointing guns everywhere, barking orders and questions at her. So engulfed in her madness, she didn't notice the officers snapping their fingers in front of her face, asking her if she was all right.

Margie had lost everything.

44.

The car was nearly out of gas by the time Jacob arrived back at the cabin in Woodstock, but that was all right. He had no intention of going anywhere else. He killed the engine but kept the headlights shining against the cabin. He unlocked the front door, stepped in, and turned on the lights.

This all ends tonight, he thought.

Jacob stood in the living room for a long time, looking around. His research was still spread out on the table in the kitchen. Pain and anger soared through him at the sight of it.

So much of his life had been wasted. All his research, obsessions, dreams, and goals. All of it had only led to death and destruction, in the name of conquering something that had haunted him for his entire life. It was all so inglorious.

Now though, that great mortal dread he had always feared suddenly didn't seem so scary anymore. In fact, it seemed like the only thing that was left for him. There was no escaping this. People were dead because of him. It was far worse to keep going.

He thought about the hole that he had started digging in the woods to bury the subjects, and suddenly he had a better alternative to dispose of them. They were all still in the basement. *Yes, a much better alternative.*

Jacob went to an equipment shack behind the cabin. He sifted through the shovels, wheelbarrows and concrete bags until he found what he was looking for: a kerosene can. He lifted it by the handle and heard the liquid inside slosh around. It would be more than enough.

Jacob stepped back into the cabin and went around pouring kerosene on as much as he could. He started in the cellar, dousing his experiments, diagrams, freezers, and tools, then poured a trail up the stairs. He splashed it all over the furniture in the living room and on his research on the kitchen table. By then the can had emptied, and the smell of the flammable liquid that would destroy his legacy drowned out the stench of decomposition and chemicals.

There was just one last thing left to do. In the bedroom was a little wooden box, a polished mahogany casket with red jewels on the lid sitting on the bureau. It had been a gift from his parents when he was sixteen years old, not long after he told them about his decision to commit to medical school. His mother had told him that he should keep his most prized possession in it.

Jacob went into the bedroom and opened the box. Within was an Avo Heritage cigar that Jacob had purchased about a week before Peter was resurrected. He had planned to sit down and smoke it when he brought Peter back, as a way of congratulating himself. However, once he did succeed, Jacob felt no desire to smoke it anymore, and the cigar had sat in its mahogany box untouched.

Now seemed like a good time to have it. Jacob took the cigar up and stuck it in his mouth. He chewed on it and took up a lighter sitting next to the box, then stepped out of the bedroom and entered the living room.

No longer would he live in fear. Jacob sat on the couch and relaxed with one leg over his knee, feeling the wet kerosene sink into his clothes. He lit the cigar, puffing it, savoring the smoke in his mouth, then clapped the lighter shut and stuck it in his pocket. Jacob stared at the ceiling, the cigar burning between his fingers, thinking over his life. Occasionally, he took a pull from the cigar, swished the smoke around from cheek to cheek, and then blew it out.

Once, when he was little, his mother had told him that through science, anything was possible. The only limit was his imagination. In Jacob's case, there was no limit. Once everything burned away, his parents would never know where his imagination had taken him. The world didn't need to see or learn about what he had discovered.

Up until now, Jacob had been lead to believe that science was the greatest force in the world—even greater than Nature itself. Yet, Nature didn't appreciate him stepping on her toes, and she retook control and punished him for it. Even the most significant accomplishments of science could never truly conquer her power, and now he was feeling her scorned wrath for his daring insult to her. The powers of Life and Death came with a rolodex of consequences. Life and Death lay nestled in Nature's bosom like young infants, and Jacob supposed that she was protective over them for reasons that he could never understand. Nobody ever would.

Jacob took one final puff of the cigar, looked at the burning tip for a few moments, and suddenly recalled what Sartre had once written in *Nausea*.

"Every existing thing is born without reason, prolongs itself out of weakness, and dies by chance."

Swiftly, Jacob pitched the cigar at the kerosene-soaked carpet. Instantly, the fire spread throughout the living room. It consumed the couch within seconds, and Jacob burned with it.

Within two minutes, the cabin became a raging bonfire. Nothing was left by the time the fire department put it out hours later. Nothing except ashes and a bunch of old, smoldering bones.

Jayson Robert Ducharme

V.
Epilogue

45.

Officer Matthew Enfield of the Manchester Police Department stood in the parking lot of the Waumbeck Warehouse on Commercial Street, where the truck of a suspect responsible for five known murders had been abandoned. He was a tall man with an upturned nose and deep-set eyes that were shadowed from the parking lot lights. Enfield hadn't been with the MPD for very long—only six months, in fact—but this was by far the most significant thing that had happened on his watch during his time on the force.

The parking lot was taped off from the public, which caused a lot of distress for the warehouse workers when they clocked out for the night. A few of the boys from the crime lab, along with a handful of Manchester police officers, scouted around the lot with their flashlights, looking for any evidence that could explain what the hell had been happening for the past few days. The only thing they found so far was a nasty-looking blood and pus trail leading from the truck to the street, but that was it. Ephraim Jessup, a pudgy mustached guy, was head of the crime lab, and he was by the truck swabbing it for prints along with an assistant.

Most of everything Officer Enfield had heard was through the grapevine, and some of it didn't make much sense to him. Enfield was never a sophisticated thinker. He approached things from a straightforward, simple perspective, but in a case like this, that sort of thinking wasn't viable.

From what he understood, the truck was rented from a place in Boston by a guy from Chicago named Jacob Abbott, all the way back in November. An investigation opened on Abbott, but so far the only thing they could find was his last place of residence two years ago, all the way in Washington, D.C. Six people were dead across two states: a mom and her kid in Methuen, Massachusetts; Trooper Bryan Parkland up by Exit 3; and finally, a little kid, her grandmother, and the prime suspect himself right here in Manchester.

A total of four officers were dispatched to the Strauss residence on 14 Piscataquog Road, traveling in two cruisers, responding to a call from the Lowell Police Department. According to Leroy Schneider, one of the officers who went inside the house, the suspect was horribly deformed.

"Looked like fucking *Night of the Living Dead* or some shit," Schneider had told Enfield at the station. "I'm telling you, it was disgusting. He stank like roadkill and you could see his goddamn skull and everything. He must have been a leper or had a bad case of syphilis."

"Always wear protection," Enfield had said to humor him. Schneider hadn't been in the mood for jokes.

"Me and Bronson went into the house because the front door was wide open and we heard this awful screaming inside," Schneider had explained. "That's when we saw it. That freak on the floor and a woman holding her dead kid. It was trippy, man. She was crying and laughing at the same time and wouldn't respond to anything we said or ordered. Once the EMTs got there, they drugged her up and carted her off to the psych unit over at Elliott. The lady looked like she had gone totally bananas."

Enfield drummed his fingers against his belt and looked around the parking lot. One of the forensic specialists knelt and focused his flashlight on something on the pavement. Enfield sighed. Was that deformed guy Abbott? What's the motive, or even the connection with the murder victims?

He supposed it wasn't his job to think too hard about it. Let the staties, the crime lab, and the chief deal with it. As far as he was concerned, his job tonight was to look tough and make sure nobody trespassed, so that's what he planned to do.

Heavy footsteps sounded behind him. Ephraim Jessup approached holding a green binder in his gloved hand.

"Enfield, look at what we found under the passenger seat of the truck."

"What is it?"

Jessup opened the binder and began flipping through the laminated pages, which glimmered under the parking lot lights. Within were pictures of dead people being cut up and sewn together, along with obituaries, autopsy reports, and a bunch of diagrams detailing all sorts of science bullshit that Enfield couldn't understand.

"This was in the truck?" Enfield asked.

Jessup nodded and closed the binder. "It was, along with a few other folders and dossiers. I don't know what to make of it. It looks like some sick mad scientist shit."

"Who was this guy?"

"I couldn't tell you." Jessup sighed. "I'm just gonna leave it for Dempsey over in the lab. Maybe he'll find something interesting in it. I'm tired."

"Wanna grab a coffee?"

"I'll think about it."

The Modern Prometheus

Jessup crossed the parking lot to a little white tent that had been pitched up at the edge of the lot. The inside glowed from battery-powered lamps, and a portable table had been set up with bagged evidence on it: a few bullets, the truck plates, a roll of duct tape, and blood swabs. Jessup took a plastic biohazard bag from a box next to the table, slipped the binder into it and sealed it. He labeled it "HUMAN EXPERIMENT DOCUMENTS" before placing it with the rest of the evidence. He took a moment to ponder all the weird things he had seen within its pages, and then stepped out of the tent.

Yeah, he thought. *Dempsey might make something out of it. Somebody will figure it out, and maybe even learn from it.*

Jessup decided to take a break, so he met up with Enfield to ask about that coffee.

May 2020 – February 2022
Salem, New Hampshire

Jayson Robert Ducharme

The Modern Prometheus

Jayson Robert Ducharme

Thank you for purchasing *The Modern Prometheus*.

If you enjoyed this book, please consider leaving a review on Amazon. Every review helps immensely. If you'd like updates on future content, free promotions, giveaways, and more, then subscribe to my newsletter at www.jaysonrobertducharme.com.

J.R.D.